Seumas
A Time Travel Romance

Dunskey Castle Book 2

JANE STAIN

DEDICATION

To Mom with love from Cher.

Thank you for giving me
Outlander and Dragonfly in Amber
way back in 1997.
And thank you for taking me to Scotland
way back in 1989.
You planted the seeds.
And look what grew.

Contents

ACKNOWLEDGMENTS

Thank you Diana Gabaldon for inventing a whole new genre of books called Time Travel Romances.

Aon (One in Gaelic)

Sasha smiled at her best friend Kelsey as the two of them waved at the BBC Scotland news crew and watched them drive away.

"If I had told you while we were at Celtic University that we would soon be in charge of a dig worthy of worldwide news —"

Kelsey smiled back at her.

"Nope, I never would have believed that."

Sasha looked out at the tower house called Dunskey Castle and used her imaginary x-ray vision to see through it to the underground palace they were digging out beneath it. She also enjoyed the ragged sea cliffs of the Scottish coastline and finally gazed across the sea at the sunset over distant Ireland. This was exactly what she had imagined she would be doing all seven years she toiled through college to get her doctorate in Celtic archaeology to make it possible.

She was so proud of herself. Her goal in life had been to escape the boring suburbs of Middle America, and at only twenty-five years old, she had already succeeded beyond her wildest dreams.

She turned back to her friend.

"I thought my face was going to crack, I was smiling so hard when you said I should go ahead and open one of the secret doors for the camera crew." She held up her phone for Kelsey to see. "My mom and my brother and my cousins and seventeen friends have already texted to say they saw me on TV."

Kelsey smiled, but it looked a little strained, and she kept glancing over across the dig site to the crew trailers, where her new kilted boyfriend Tavish was on the phone.

Sasha saw that all the rest of the construction workers were goofing around, now that the day was over. None of them was wearing a kilt. And they were all real Scots, while Kelsey had known her boyfriend back in the States before she went off to college. What was up with him wearing that kilt? Hardly practical for construction work.

Kelsey answered her in a soft voice while still watching Tavish.

"Yeah, my mom and everyone back home texted me, too. I gave Gisa both of our numbers, and she promised to text us a link where we can watch ourselves on a repeat of the broadcast."

"Good."

Watching the construction crew guys play gave

Sasha pangs of homesickness for the seventeen friends she'd made at Celtic University in the short three months she'd been a professor there. But she was good at making friends fast. Maybe she'd go over and join the guys.

The oddness of their activity made her pause, though. They were playing this dangerous he-man game where they tried to lift up a log by the end and hold the log so that it was vertical in the air, then let it fall down in front of themselves. Guys were so weird.

Sasha flinched as one of the guys accidentally dropped the log sideways. It came crashing down to the ground, bounced off one end, bounced off the other end, and would have hit Tavish if one of the guys hadn't pushed him out of the way.

Unfortunately, Tavish was so busy on his phone, he didn't realize why the guy had pushed him, and he fell, landing on his face on a rock. He got up and shoved the guy back, but some others came over and they appeared to be sorting it out, thank goodness.

"What's so important on the phone that he almost got killed over it?"

Kelsey sighed.

"Did I ever tell you he has a twin brother?"

"He does?"

"Yeah, I thought I'd never see Tavish again — let alone be with him again — so I didn't explain his family dynamics. But among a slew of other issues that we need to explain to you once we get a chance, Tavish has a twin. His name is Tomas, and he's being stupid. Tavish is stuck here and wants his brother to come visit him, and Tomas won't come."

Sasha gave her friend a sideways hug as they stood there watching the guys, who in no time at all had started a new game: throwing their knives into the big log the one guy had dropped, which was now wedged between two boulders ten feet away from them.

Behind her, she heard the voice of Mr. Blair, the property owner and thus her and Kelsey's client.

"Ye lasses use my trailer again this night, and I'll stay in toon again. I've texted ye the link tae the web thingy where ye can look over the trailers they have and pick the one ye want. If ye let me ken this night, maybe we can even have it oot here tomorrow, though that is Sunday, so maybe not till Monday."

He shook both of their hands as he said this, and then they walked him to his car, which was parked in front of his trailer.

He had been Kelsey's client first, so she spoke for the two of them.

"Thank you so much, Mr. Blair. We'll pick something out within the hour and let you know, so that you can call the trailer guy before it gets late."

Mr. Blair nodded and smiled at them as he got in his car, then drove off.

Sasha went on into the trailer, calling over her shoulder at Kelsey just before the door closed.

"Guess we'd better get to it. Come on, Kelsey. They won't quit goofing around until dark, and that's a good hour yet."

While she waited for Kelsey to come in, she answered her texts. The ones from her family were all gooey, even the one from her brother, but some of her friends had sent screenshots of her on TV and doctored them with an app. One made her long red hair look like it was on fire. Another made her look like a lion, about to eat the camera. They were funny, and she was laughing out loud when Kelsey came in.

"Okay Butterfly, tear yourself away from your many fans long enough to flit over here and help me pick out our trailer."

As it always did, Kelsey's nickname for her made Sasha laugh even louder.

"I'll be there in a second."

The two of them had just texted Mr. Blair their choice of a two-bedroom, two-bathroom trailer in three complementary shades of blue when there was a knock on the door and they heard Tavish's voice.

"It's me, Kel. And Gus is here too, with Tuffy."

"Come on in," Kelsey called out to them.

Gus and Tuffy turned out to be a big old Scottish construction worker and his tiny little dog, whom he cradled like a baby. Tavish had brought a case of champagne, and the five of them partied, toasting the news exposure and Mr. Blair's meeting with a publicist on Monday with the intention of bringing tourists to the area so that he could turn a handy profit— and pay them all well.

~*~

The next morning Sasha came out of the bathroom after her shower wearing the professional suit she'd put on her credit card, whose bill made her oh, so thankful to have a better-paying job.

And Kelsey was dressed in old fashioned Scottish garb: long plaid overdress in red and green, green blouse with huge billowy sleeves, worn leather belt over it all with pouches and a cup and other implements hanging from it by leather cords.

Sasha stopped in her tracks.

"What's with the outfit?"

Kelsey brought over to the table a large pitcher of suspicious-looking orange liquid.

"You'll see. Will you pour the mimosas while I finish making the omelets?"

Sasha took the pitcher and poured, secretly glad there was more champagne. She hadn't thought this place would be so far from everything. She'd need to stock the fridge better. And find out if there was going to be a problem.

"Okay, but won't Mr. Blair be upset if he smells this on our breath?"

Kelsey laughed at the stove.

"Nah, they're more relaxed over here about alcohol, especially when you don't work for a university — much more so than back home in the US. We don't usually drink with breakfast, though, but we're still in a celebrating mood, so why not use up the rest of the champagne?"

Sasha brought over two glasses and clinked with Kelsey before she chugged hers.

"I'll drink to that!"

They laughed.

Tavish joined them, and they all sat down and dug in. The food was great — and so were the mimosas. They passed a few minutes just eating and drinking and making appreciative noises.

But Sasha couldn't keep quiet for long.

"Tavish, I know there's something going on today, because Kelsey's dressed up too, but why do you always wear a kilt? I mean, it looks great and all, but you aren't on stage. You're here to do a job. And none of the other guys wear kilts on the job. Am I right?" She ate the last bite of her omelet, eagerly awaiting his response.

"About that." Kelsey chugged the rest of her third mimosa.

Tavish had already chugged his fourth drink.

"We talked about it, and the easiest thing is if we just show you why I wear my kilt all the time."

Sasha poured her fourth mimosa while she gave them her best excitedly curious face.

"Okay. Are you going to get up and do a little dance, Tavish?"

Tavish laughed.

"The day has only just begun, so you never know. You might even do a little dance before this is over. In fact, I can't wait to see the look on your face."

Kelsey playfully hit his chest with the back of her hand and rolled her eyes.

"Sasha, there's all kinds of reasons we need to show you this — and before your dirty mind goes into full gear, all of them are professional."

Wow, they were serious. Sasha downed the rest of the pitcher and stood up, wiping her mouth with the back of her hand and then wiping the lipstick off her hand with her napkin.

"All right, so show me already."

Kelsey started to go into the other room, but Tavish grabbed her arm playfully and pulled her back.

"We'll only stay a few minutes. Don't worry about her clothes this time."

He got his long plaid cloak from the chair and held it out.

"Here, Sasha. Just throw this around yourself."

He looked at her shoes and shrugged. It was the first time a straight man had ever looked at her shoes.

She looked down at them herself, smiling at the head rush and reaching out a hand to stabilize herself on a chair. She'd known yesterday's rain would make the ground muddy, so she'd sprayed Scotch Gard on her knee-high leather boots.

She raised one eyebrow at Tavish and turned her head sideways, but she took his cloak and threw it around her shoulders dramatically. Then she gave Kelsey an incredulous look, exaggerated for effect.

"What, is there a costume party and nobody told me?"

"Even better," Kelsey said with a huge grin, heading out the door.

Sasha and Tavish went out after her, and they all headed over toward the root cellar of the old tower house.

Kelsey stumbled and laughed as she turned to walk backwards, then studied Sasha for a moment.

"Yeah, if we only go for a few minutes, you should be okay if you keep that cloak on. I can't wait for you to see this."

Mr. Blair's car pulled up then.

Kelsey wrinkled her nose in that way that meant she'd been caught being naughty. Interesting. She and Tavish looked at each other and had a silent conversation. The upshot was that they were going to stay and talk to Mr. Blair for a moment and hope it didn't ruin their plans, whatever those were.

More curious by the moment.

Sasha smiled and waved at Mr. Blair as he walked over.

After waving back, he pointed at a cut Tavish had on his face, from falling yesterday during the crew's odd game.

"I can give ye shaving lessons if ye hae that much trouble, lad."

Tavish put a hand to his cut with an odd look on his face as if he was surprised there was something there and smiled at Mr. Blair.

"Verra funny."

Mr. Blair looked at Kelsey's outfit appreciatively and then glanced at Sasha's cloak.

"Good, good, go on doon and take the photos we talked aboot, Kelsey. I'll hae the men get yer area cleared oot for when yer trailer arrives today."

Sasha felt a little disappointed at hearing they were just going to take publicity pictures, but she supposed it made sense. The prospect of getting their new trailer here today was great, though. No more sleeping in the living room, and she would have her own bathroom. Two women sharing a bathroom was a hardship. There was never enough room for her makeup.

Sasha and Kelsey spoke at the same time.

"That's great news, Mr. Blair."

"Thank you, Mr. Blair."

He smiled and nodded and moved on toward where all the construction crew were standing around drinking coffee and laughing, apparently waiting for him.

Gus waved, and Sasha waved back. Maybe later she would go over and see if she could join in on any of the gang's shenanigans.

Tavish held open the trap door to the root cellar while Sasha and Kelsey went down the ladder in their skirts.

Using her phone as a flashlight, Sasha went over to the secret door she had opened on TV.

"Should we take the pictures right here? This is one of the heavily featured places in the broadcast, so most people should recognize it, if they saw us on TV. That should be a pretty good tourist draw, don't you think?"

Tavish and Kelsey shrugged at each other for a moment, having another one of those silent conversations before Kelsey answered.

"Yeah, let's go ahead and take the pictures. Tavish, go stand with Sasha — and leave room for me. I'll set my phone up here on this ledge and use my timer app."

Sasha couldn't quite shake the feeling that something was off as they took about a dozen pictures, and then she was sure of it when Kelsey opened the secret door instead of following when Sasha started to climb the ladder again.

Kelsey called up to Sasha as she and Tavish entered the formerly secret corridor, hollowed out from solid rock. Her tone was deliberately casual, but Sasha could hear an undertone of excitement — and something else she couldn't quite identify.

"Come on, Sasha. We still need to show you something."

Sasha had been in the secret corridor with the news crew yesterday, so she wondered why her knees trembled as she went back down the ladder and followed Tavish and Kelsey down the corridor to a three-way intersection. As she had yesterday, she marveled at all the Celtic runes engraved in the walls. They were lacy and beautiful, but more so, they imparted the wisdom of the Druids — the priests of the ancient Celts. She and Kelsey had learned to read them in college.

She was about to speak up and warn Tavish and Kelsey that they were walking right into a wall when it disappeared and they walked through where it had been and turned to make sure she was following.

She did follow.

"How many mimosas did I drink?"

Kelsey sounded amused.

"I think you had five, and we all chugged our last one, remember?"

As Sasha ruminated over this, she followed the others down another corridor similar to the one off the root cellar — except this one dead ended.

Before she could ask what the heck they were doing here, Kelsey grabbed her in a hug. Good thing she had, too, because Sasha got so dizzy she almost fell down. But unlike other times she'd had a few too many and gotten dizzy, this dizziness kept getting more and more intense until it seemed like the cave was spinning around her.

The dizziness finally subsided, but Sasha was having some kind of visual problem, because the stone walls looked — cleaner. So did the floor and the ceiling.

Kelsey held her in a sideways hug and started walking her back down the corridor again.

"The dizziness will go away, I promise. I don't want to wait, though. I've just got to show you this."

Sasha imagined so, because it was turning out to be quite a lot of trouble to show her whatever this was. She hoped it was worth it. At least she didn't feel nauseated.

She figured they must be involved in live action roleplaying, because Tavish walked with them on Kelsey's other side, talking nonsense.

"There's only one place you really have to be careful, and that's at the door to the tower where Brian the Druid is imprisoned. We'll show you where he is, just so you know to be careful when you go near there."

Sasha stopped walking.

"Brian the Druid?"

Tavish laughed.

"Yeah, that's what I said."

Kelsey's arm around her was shaking, she was so excited.

"Okay, once we leave this part of the corridor, we'll need to speak in Gaelic. And we won't be able to talk about certain things until we get back. No one but Tavish or a Druid can see past the illusion of the cave wall into this corridor, so this corridor is a pretty safe place to run to for refuge from anyone else. Meet here if we get separated."

Sasha laughed.

"Meet here if we get separated? You sound like my mother."

Tavish smiled.

"I'm glad you're having a good time. I can't wait to see your face once we get to the surface. We'll just go have a look around and come right back, this first time. Those mimosas will probably help you out, and you might even feel like dancing that jig."

Sasha threw her arms up in the air and gave them her best 'well come on then' look.

Kelsey turned around at the opening out of the corridor, chuckling a little at Sasha's frustration as she got out a lighter and lit three torches.

"Okay, put away your phone. Now take this torch. We're switching to Gaelic in just a second, but I'd better tell you this real quick. The only reason we came here in the first place was because the druids sent Tavish here to get a mag— ... a special artifact for them. You can't trust any of the druids, Sasha. It's not just Brian. They're all extremely dangerous."

Okay. So they wanted to play medieval dangerous druid games that involved speaking Gaelic. Fine. She played along, switching to the Gaelic she had been taught at Celtic University just as the three of them walked out of the corridor into the three-way intersection.

"Verra well. I willna fash any o the druids. Am I needing tae run when I see one, or are ye taking me tae a druid dress-up ball?"

But she didn't even hear their responses, because at the far end of the corridor facing her — wearing a kilt like Tavish's and at least three weapons, not to mention sporting a mane of long fiery red hair — was the most gorgeous specimen of a man Sasha had ever seen.

Dhà (2)

Sasha knew she was staring, but she couldn't help herself. The man looked like an old statue of a warrior come to life. There was not an ounce of fat on him. His muscles showed detail like those of old master statues chiseled out of marble. Unlike Tavish, who knew he looked good in a kilt and flaunted it, this man wore his kilt — as well as a coordinating linen shirt, an arisade, and heavy handmade leather boots — as if it were normal clothes. He had a huge sword strapped to his back, and the scuffs and small cuts all over it attested to the fact that he used it and didn't just wear it for show. His long red hair was tied in a loose ponytail with a leather cord, and his head was otherwise bare, his face positively glowing with health and vigor in the light of the torch he carried.

With an appreciative smile, he was looking her over from head to toe also, while absentmindedly speaking to Tavish in perfectly accented Gaelic with a deep rich voice that she would bet was great for singing.

"I see ye hae found yer sporran, as wull as a lass, whom I'm guessing is another clanswoman o yers."

Wow, this was one elaborate role-playing game. Sasha pulled the cloak around her a little more tightly. She'd only just met him, and she felt like she had let this gorgeous hunk of a man down somehow. She didn't want to disappoint him by letting him see that she hadn't gone to any trouble to look historic.

She gave Kelsey a look that she meant to say, 'Why did you and Tavish have to be in such a hurry to get here? Didn't you mention clothes I could have put on?'

Kelsey cringed a little and shrugged at her.

Sasha couldn't see Tavish, only hear his voice responding. And Tavish sounded frustrated. She could almost hear him changing plans in his mind, because of running into this man.

But upon looking back at the man, she decided she didn't care that much.

The guy was such great eye candy. The more she looked at him, the more she was impressed by how authentic his clothing was. New details kept leaping out at her: a rip in his sleeve that had been hand mended, the hand stitching around the collar of his shirt, the way his boots were buttoned shut instead of zipped or tied.

But mostly he was just so darn good looking she couldn't tear her eyes away. And unlike how Tavish would've taken the attention, this man had the decency to pretend he didn't notice she was staring at him. Which impressed her all the more, making her want to know more about him.

Meanwhile, Tavish was talking.

"Aye, I did find it. Thank ye for asking. Sasha, this is Seumas (Shaymus), my sparring buddy and fellow guard here at Laird Malcomb's castle, not to mention being the laird's nephew."

Seumas bowed to her in a way that made her feel honored rather than entertained. And the look in his eyes made her heart race.

And then Tavish was introducing her, and she found herself standing up straight and raising her chin in a way that would honor Seumas back.

"Seumas, this is Sasha, and aye, she is also my clanswoman. It's her foremaist time away from home, sae she wull need a bit o understanding and looking after. Kelsey and I are sharing that responsibility, and mayhap ye will help us."

Puzzled, Sasha looked over at Tavish, and then at Kelsey. With her eyes, she tried her best to ask them why Tavish was lying and saying it was her first time away from home. And then she put her hand on her hip and raised her eyebrows, doing her best to tell them they'd better have a good reason to say she needed looking after.

But they couldn't keep her attention. Smiling tightly to keep the drool inside her mouth, Sasha turned to Seumas and held out her hand for him to shake.

"Wull met."

But Seumas didn't take her hand. No, he awkwardly looked over at Tavish, apparently waiting for permission to touch her. They were taking this game way too far, and she was about to say so when Kelsey moved in front of them all and spoke up in a take-charge way.

"Tavish, I think mayhap we'd better hurry up and show her the castle toon," she looked pointedly at Seumas, "all things considered."

But Sasha was looking mostly at Seumas and Tavish, and she saw the subtle look that passed between them just before Seumas reverently took her hand in his, saying something innocuous like she had. It could've been 'well met.' She didn't really know.

Because as soon as Seumas touched her, Sasha had a vision.

They were outside, and Seumas was lying down on the ground, his face stoically trying to hide pain. She was looking at his shoulder, which was red and blistering.

And that was it. As quickly as the vision had come, it was gone. She tried to remember all the details she could, but it was difficult because she had never seen the location before, and it was dark in the vision. Not night, just deep shade. There was some sort of structure around them — not a building, but something she couldn't define.

Seumas was still holding her hand, giving her a concerned look.

She must have been unresponsive for a moment. Pretty sure her vision wasn't part of the game, she told the first lie that came to mind, proud of herself for sticking to Gaelic as instructed, even under really odd circumstances.

"Sorry, I just had the oddest sense o déjà vu. I'm wull now."

That seemed to placate Seumas. He nodded in understanding.

But Sasha could see that Kelsey wasn't fooled. Giving her a knowing look, her friend clapped her hands and started walking up the corridor away from whence they'd come.

"Wull, now that ye two hae met, let's go on up tae the castle toon and show Sasha aroond."

Tavish nodded sideways to Seumas, who held out his hand in a gesture that indicated Sasha should go ahead of him and follow Kelsey, so she did.

The whole way out along the corridor — which seemed a lot longer on the way out that it had on the way in — she was hyper aware of Seumas behind her. Her back and butt tingled with the awareness of his presence as if they were bidding him in like odd magical magnets.

Her attention was briefly drawn away from him when she realized they were leaving a different way than they'd come in. She almost said something, and then she wasn't sure if it would fit into the game or not, so she kept quiet — which had always been difficult for her.

And then they were outside, and everything looked, smelled, and sounded different. Really different. Too different for a mere game. A gigantic castle loomed to her left, and it wasn't the old tower house, but something truly formidable. An entire town surrounded the castle, bustling with people and animals and wagons. All the trailers were gone. There was no sign of any of the construction crew. It was like a different… century.

She walked up and got in Kelsey's face.

"What the hell's going on, Kelsey? Where did all this stuff come from, and all these people? They weren't here ten minutes ago when we went down into the dig."

Kelsey hugged her tight and stroked her back, as if soothing her. But she whispered in her ear.

"We've traveled back in time, Sasha. Near as I can tell, we're in the thirteenth century. I wanted to tell you we were going to time travel, but you wouldn't have believed me. This is how we know so much about what's in the dig. Well, part of how we know, anyway. We didn't mean for Seumas to join us. Now do you see why we have to pretend like you've never been away from home before and this is your first time in the big city?"

Big city? This wasn't even a town, really, just a bunch of houses and a huge castle.

A castle.

There hadn't been a castle on this site since…

Kelsey pulled away a bit, looking at Sasha with caution in her eyes.

Sasha sat dazed, blown away by what had happened. As far-fetched as what Kelsey said was, it was the only explanation for what Sasha saw around her. Mostly the castle. It was … huge and very real. People were going in and out of it, or she might have thought it was a movie set. But that was far from the only convincing detail. There was not a mechanical sound to be heard, nor the smell of any exhaust. And the distinct scent of manure lingered where these had been.

She'd traveled back in time! She couldn't even form words, her mind was exploding with so many implications.

But she quietly nodded her agreement to the farce.

Once she wrapped her mind around the situation, she couldn't help getting a big smile on her face. This was so cool. Already she understood a thousand times as much about the dig site as she had when she woke up this morning, and she hadn't even walked around yet.

Kelsey smiled big as well, switching back to Gaelic and speaking aloud once more, leading Sasha down the street.

"Sae this is the toon that has sprung up aroond Laird Malcomb's castle. We hae all the shops: blacksmith, fletcher, weaver, cobbler, ye name it. It's a marketplace for the surrounding area, and as ye see, folk bring their crops in tae sell, as wull as prepared food and other crafts."

Sasha could feel Seumas close behind her once more, almost burning her backside with his warm presence. Just to make sure it wasn't her imagination, she turned and looked.

He was in the middle of conversation with Tavish, but his eyes met hers, and he gave her a tentative smile. It made his face light up so that he was even more handsome.

She smiled back at him, aware that she was flirting with a man she had nothing in common with and too buzzed on mimosas to care whether it was a good idea. Tavish and Kelsey seemed to trust him, and that was good enough for her.

Kelsey was talking still.

"And this is Captain Donnell. Captain, this is our clanswoman Sasha. 'Tis her foremaist time tae market, and we're showing her aroond."

This woke Sasha up from her stare at Seumas. Some part of her buzzed brain knew she'd best show her manners when being introduced to someone, especially a captain. She turned back around to see a man she could only describe as a pirate — minus the eye patch, the peg leg, and the parrot.

He had his thumbs hooked into his jerkin and he was rocking back on his heels, smiling at her even though he was addressing Tavish.

"Wull now, another braw keekin lass ye hae brought intae toon, eh Tavish?"

Sasha felt Seumas coming up close behind her.

Captain Donnell must've noticed that, because he addressed the man.

"Och, and it seems this one is taken as wull, eh Seumas?"

But Seumas surprised her with his smoothness, ignoring the comment and changing the subject.

"Wull met, Captain. Where are ye off tae next? Must be someplace pure special, for we are na in line tae guard ye this time."

Captain Donnell threw back his head and laughed.

"Aye, 'tis off up and aroond tae Norway I am a few days hence, muckle tae craking a steid for the likes o ye. Nah, for real sure, the laird telt me tae keep ye back from it this time. I dinna ken why."

He gave both Tavish and Seumas hearty pats on the back and headed off down the street past them.

They looked at each other for a moment of deep questioning, but eventually shrugged it off.

Kelsey was pointing out this shop and that vendor

cart, but Sasha wasn't paying much attention. Seumas had insinuated himself alongside her somehow, and the backs of their hands brushed every now and then, thoroughly distracting her.

Kelsey's tour guide routine only intruded on Sasha's distraction when introductions were in order — but the introductions came all too often for Sasha's liking.

"Och, and there are the guards I telt ye aboot. Dubh 'n' Luthais, this is our clanswoman Sasha. It's her foremaist time tae any castle, and we're showing her aroond."

These two merely nodded and smiled as they passed by, thank goodness. Because Seumas was making small talk with her.

"Is the castle toon as grand as ye thought it would be, lass?"

She turned on her charm a little, answering as truthfully as she dared.

"I hadna given any thought tae it, in truth, but there are far more folk here than I expected."

He gave her a sympathetic smile and nodded as his sturdy legs carried him along the road, his kilt bouncing in step along with his long red hair. And then oddly, he stepped to the side of the road, pulling her along with him and bowing his head slightly.

Sasha looked up to see what the matter was, but all she saw was a rather well-dressed kilted Scot among a bunch of hangers on — looking right at her and coming their way.

Also off to the side and bowing slightly, tour guide Kelsey spoke up again right before the well-dressed man reached them.

"Laird Malcomb, may I present our clanswoman

Sasha?"

The laird gave Sasha an appraising look, spending extra time looking at her Celtic University ring, and she found herself standing up as straight as she could. Should she have removed the ring when she put her phone away? She was pretty sure it would suit any period when handcrafted rings were possible.

Seumas moved in close beside her, while still leaving his sword arm free.

"Are ye wull, Uncle? Ye dinna seem at all yerself. Can Tavish get ye anything?"

The laird turned a displeased gaze on Seumas, and Sasha feared for his life. Other people had moved off to the side of the road too, also bowing their heads, and it reminded her of when cars pulled over because they heard a siren.

But then the laird gazed around at the crowd and seemed to remember himself.

"Thank ye for presenting yer ... clanswoman," he said to Kelsey. And then he turned to Sasha with a big jovial smile on his face that didn't make it to his eyes. "Well come tae Caer Uchtred."

Being American and having not watched local TV here at university, Sasha had never seen a lord before — let alone been introduced to one. She inclined her head the same way he had and then began to raise her face to his again in order to address him. She thought this was the polite thing to do. After all, her mother had always said, 'look at me when I'm talking to you.'

But Seumas put his arm around her shoulders and gently pressed her forward a bit, until her face was lowered once more.

And all hell broke loose in her body. If the mimosas were giving her a warm feeling, that was nothing compared to the fire that blazed in her at having so much body contact with him. Did he feel it, too?

She had started fanning herself with her hand when a little girl no more than six years old appeared in front of Sasha's face, looking her over with a skeptical and discerning eye. The girl had a proportionally sized marketing basket on her arm, and she was dressed in a small version of adult clothes like Kelsey's: plaid woolen overdress and solid linen blouse.

"Is this yer wife, Seumas? How come wasna she with ye afore? Dinna ye like her?"

Seumas smiled at the girl.

"I am na able tae speak tae ye just at the moment, Deirdre, seeing as how Laird Malcomb demands my attention, but I wull be with ye presently, if ye dinna mind."

Deirdre stepped back a bit and put her hands on her hips, shaking her head no.

"Nay, I dinna mind at all. Go ahead and blether tae Laird Malcomb. I shall wait."

But Laird Malcomb took one look at Deirdre and went away down the road past them, scowling at all of his sycophants. Good riddance to bad rubbish.

In the background, Sasha heard Kelsey and Tavish discussing him.

"He was sae kind when last I did see him."

"Aye, he is normally verra kind. I dinna ken what's come ower him. Mayhap a severe threat tae the castle militarily. 'Tis the only thing I ken that would make him sae... unpleasant."

But meanwhile, Sasha and Seumas were talking to Deirdre — or rather, she was talking to them.

"Ye shouldna leave yer wife oot in the land when ye come tae the castle, Seumas. Wives like it at the castle. When Da was aroond, Maw was always telling him how she liked it here at the castle and was sae glad they were na oot in the land anymore. And I ken when yer brother Alfred marries Maw, he will let her bide here at the castle, for he's the laird's nephew, and laird's nephews bide at the castle. Aw, ye are the laird's nephew tae, then. How come was he sae mean tae ye?"

Seumas stood and gave Sasha his arm to pull herself up with, which she gladly did, relishing the feel of his strong muscle under her hand just as much as the firm support he provided. Yum.

He reached out with his other hand to mess up the little girl's hair, but she ducked, making him chuckle.

"I dinna ken how come Laird Malcomb is being sae mean this day, but I'm verra glad that ye came along and made him go away."

Deirdre stood up straight and gave him a single nod.

"You're verra wull come. I can dae that anytime."

Sasha met Seumas's eyes, and they shared a smile in appreciation of how adorable the little girl was. Sasha lingered there in the smile as long as she could, admiring the set of Seumas's light blue eyes, the chisel of his cheekbones, the lustrousness of his long red hair...

Kelsey made her way back up to the front of their group and pointed out this sausage vendor and that cooper shop as she led them farther along the road through the castle town market. It made a circle around the castle, and they'd already gone halfway around, the town was so small.

All in all, it was like a carnival at home, and Sasha loved it. Every now and then, she would see a table of wares that especially attracted her, and she would stop to handle and admire them. She stopped at a table full of small handmade wooden flutes, picked out one that looked like the recorder she used to play as a child, and put it to her lips.

Without thinking, she ripped twice through "Jimmy Crack Corn and I Don't Care" while bending forward and back and dancing around the way she used to when she was a kid. She smiled and hammed it up in front of a small crowd that had gathered, stomping their feet and clapping their hands along with the music she was playing.

But then something small was behind her when she stepped backward. She lost her balance, teetered for a second, and then fell — smack in the middle of a huge mud puddle with a splash. Water soaked clear through her clothes all along her backside, and the chill autumn wind made her shiver.

Little Deirdre was jumping up and down with her hands over her ears, crying, and then she ran over and grabbed Sasha's arm and started pulling her, as if she could get her up on her feet again.

"I'm sae sorry, Seumas! Sae sorry. Maw has clothes yer wife can wear till these get cleaned. Come ower tae oor house afore she catches her death o cauld. Och, I'm sae, sae sorry!"

JANE STAIN

Trì (3)

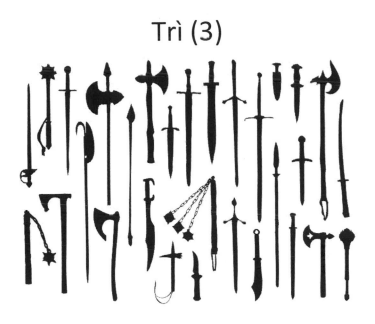

While he unfastened his brooch to loosen his arisade, Seumas gaped in dismay at the site of Sasha soaked through in mud in this shivering wind. Moments earlier, she had been so lively and joyful. That had suited her much more. The sun would go down soon, and already it was cold. Still, he gave Eileen's daughter a kind look. She hadn't meant any harm, and she was just a bairn.

"Thank ye, Deirdre, but I shall help Sasha up."

Still crying, the wee lassie dropped Sasha's hand and backed up with a sniffle.

The small crowd that had gathered to hear Sasha play the flute dispersed as quickly as it had formed, with nary a word in between. The vendors were starting to close their shops and stalls.

Deirdre picked up the flute Sasha had been playing — which had flown out of her hand and landed on dry ground, but was no doubt now a used item — and gave it back to Raild, who smiled at her and then looked expectantly at Seumas.

"Give me a moment, wull ye now?" he said to Raild while grabbing first Sasha's hand and then her elbow and then her shoulder, getting her to her feet as quickly as possible while removing first her sopping wet cloak and then her strange muddy tunic so that he could wrap his arisade tightly over her wet shirt and hug her to himself to keep her as warm as could be in the whipping wind.

Once this was done, he dug a copper out of his pouch and handed it to the craftsman in exchange for the flute, which he handed to Sasha.

"Thank ye," she said, her teeth all a chatter while she put it in a small leather bag she'd been carrying under her cloak. Something blue and shiny was in there, and he made a mental note to ask her what it was, later when they were warm.

He felt a bit of guilt at the pleasure he took from the way her body felt against his while he clung to her tightly — but he only did so to keep her warm. Her friend Kelsey came over at first, visibly wanting to take over the keep-warm duty, but Tavish held her back.

"She's had a fall, Kelsey. Let Seumas hold her up." He pulled her around to face him and gave her a tender look, caressing her face. "I fear ye are na strong enough tae dae sae."

Kelsey relented, and then something passed between the two women. Seumas couldn't see Sasha's face, but Kelsey blinked one eye at her with a smile that said they were having fun.

Good. He was having fun, too.

As the five of them hurried over to Eileen's house — which thankfully wasn't far, it was getting so cold — he wondered what his chances were with Sasha, even as he held her close, gazing at her fine featured face, her shining red hair, and her tall willowy figure that made muddy clothes and a man's arisade look braw.

She was clearly a high-ranking member of Tavish's MacGregor clan. She was confident, accustomed to the respect of all, and he detected her ability to command. Her clothing was fine, and her boots finer. She knew how to play at least one musical instrument. Her hands were smooth as silk, and her face smoother still. Her laugh came readily, without a care in the world. She hadn't ever worked in the fields. No, her father was wealthy enough to keep her away from toil. And wealthy fathers wanted wealthy husbands for their daughters.

And what did he have to offer her? He was the younger son of the laird's widowed sister. His older brother Alfred was captain of the guard and had some status in the town, but Seumas was just a rank-and-file soldier. He didn't even have rooms at the castle like his brother did, let alone a house, but slept in the barracks.

Sure, he could go out in the land and build a house, but he had no men to take with him to defend it nor to work the land — and anyhow, he had already discerned that Sasha was too fine a lady to live out in the land.

Would her clan take him in? Mayhap, if Tavish vouched for him. Howsoever, after months of almost constant companionship, he didn't even know what position Tavish held in his clan. Oddly, Tavish never spoke of it, which was just one strange thing among many he had only lately noticed about the man he'd quite enjoyed being on guard duty with.

And that reminded him.

"Tavish?"

"Aye?"

"How did ye come intae the tunnel doon tae the stone docks with yer two clanswomen when ye were meant tae be searching for yer lost sporran?"

He had the man. Now it would come down to 'put up or what for.'

The MacGregor — if that was indeed his clan — was as good a fighter as they came. Up to now, there had been no one Seumas would rather have guarding his back. Howsoever, it had lately come to Seumas's attention that Tavish was always coming in and out of one particular tunnel down the dock way at the strangest times, and now twice in the past few days he'd come out with women he claimed were in his clan.

It stank the way fish do.

But the man just shrugged, not saying anything at all in his defense.

If he hadn't saved Seumas's life and livelihood more than once, the two of them would be having words. As it was, Seumas's trust in the man was wearing thin. His guard was starting to come up between them. The man had secrets, and because they involved Seumas's home, they were his business. Later. For now, he would enjoy the company of the beautiful Sasha.

Deirdre opened the door for them all and yelled

into the house.

"Maw! I knockit Seumas's wife ower and she's all coverit in mud and all wet and they're all here right now and she needs some dry clothes and ye have tae help her!"

Eileen came around the center fireplace, brushing flour off her hands onto her apron.

He needed to stop this rumor before it spread.

"Eileen, this is Sasha. She isna my wife, but rather another o Tavish's clan come tae visit. Sasha, this is Eileen, one o our master weavers. Kelsey has apprenticed with her."

Eileen smiled in greeting at Kelsey and then spoke to Sasha while she chased her smaller three children off this side of the hearth, where they were having a grand game of storm the castle.

"Oh, ye poor thing. Here, sit doon at the fire while I find ye some dry clothes." She seated Sasha on the hearth, pulling a blanket off the chair and tucking it over Sasha's legs before she hurried into the bedroom.

Clucking just like a doting grandma, Deirdre did her best to finish tucking Sasha in, then shooed her younger brothers and sister in a fair imitation of their mother.

"Aodh! Niall! Sile! Ye wee bairns canna be in the way, I tell ye. Sit and play ower there while ye let us grown ones have oor talk."

Sasha giggled at that — unlike Kelsey, who was too preoccupied with Tavish. Or perhaps she just didn't like children much. Frowning at Kelsey in disapproval, Seumas sat down next to Sasha, taking both of her hands in his and chafing them, just to warm them, mind.

But Kelsey walked over with Tavish close beside her and held out her hand to help Sasha up.

"Sasha, come on, let's go."

Tavish nodded.

"Aye, 'tis time we were on oor way." Inexplicably, he wiped at a sore on his face and then looked at his finger to see if blood came off, which it didn't, as the sore had scabbed recently. Nonetheless, he pointed the sore out to Sasha as if it had some deep meaning. "We hae tae speak to someone ... at the castle, ye ken?"

What in the world did they mean? Kelsey was intended to stay here with Eileen before Maw insisted she stay in the castle last night because of her fall into the sea, God bless her. Was Kelsey so attached to the castle that she wanted to hurry away from the home of the woman who had taken her in as apprentice so old as five and twenty?

And who would need to speak to Tavish? He was a guard, and he was currently in the company of himself, the brother of the captain of the guard, fool for a man. New love must have addlepated the two of them.

Thankfully, Sasha had more sense than they.

"I am na rushing off intae the cauld wind in these wet clothes, and I certainly am na rushing off withoot the clothes ye brought me in. 'Twould be different had ye allowed me tae change, as ye did, Kelsey." She and Kelsey stared at each other a moment, and Kelsey looked away first. Sasha grunted. "Ye two go on, if ye must go and speak to someone. I wull bide here till ye get back."

Seumas put his arm over Sasha's shoulders and held his arisade tighter around her while also leaning her back toward the fire.

"Aye." He looked to Tavish. "Go on and dae yer errand. I can tell it's weighing on ye, whatever secret it is. Yer clanswoman is under my protection while yer gone. Dinna fash."

Kelsey and Tavish whispered among themselves in strangely accented English, and he thought he caught something like 'no time will pass' before they reluctantly agreed to leave Sasha with him for the time it took to walk up into the castle and back. He had thought Tavish was a better friend, and hoped love had just addlepated him — even as all the man's secrets started to weigh on Seumas.

Tavish took Kelsey by the waist and escorted her to the door, turning over his shoulder to address Seumas.

"Ye must look after her, ye ken?" He sighed and gave Seumas an especially appealing look with his eyes, then moved them quickly over to Sasha and back. "She does na ken she needs looking after."

"Aye," Seumas told the man as adamantly as he could without showing the anger that had started to brew at Tavish's lack of faith in him over so trivial an amount of time. What could happen anyhow, with Eileen and all the bairns watching the two of them?

At the same time, Kelsey looked at Sasha once more.

"Dinna go anywhere. To ye, we wull be right back."

What a confusing comment. Something was going on.

But Sasha seemed to have as little patience for the two of them as he did. She made a shooing gesture with her hand.

"Go on, already."

Deirdre made the same shooing gesture at Tavish and Kelsey.

"We ken how tae dry off a wet lass. Dinna fash."

While Kelsey and Tavish shuffled uncertainly out the front door, Sasha laughed and grabbed ahold of Deirdre and hugged her, and then Aodh, Niall, and Sile came running over for hugs too, which Sasha was giving generously when Eileen came back with an armful of clothing.

Sasha saw the clothing and let go of the children, standing up and putting the wet muddy blanket on the hearth so that she could accept the clothing from Eileen.

She held the clothes out away from her soaked body so that they wouldn't get muddy and looked around helplessly for someplace to change.

"Thank ye ever sae kindly."

Why didn't she just go into the bedroom? Houses couldn't be so different out in the MacGregor lands than they were here, could they?

The children were starting to fuss, a different one pulling at Eileen's skirts every time she turned around.

"When dae we eat, Maw?"

"I thought ye were making supper."

"Why dae we hae people over if they keep ye from cooking, Maw?"

Visibly concerned about getting supper into them, Eileen went back around to the kitchen side of the hearth and came back with a big pot of clear broth so everyone could at least have a nice hot drink while waiting for her to cook. Squab broth, if his nose served him right. She had set it down on her large round supper table before Seumas could get there to help her. Already she was off walking around to the kitchen side of the fire again — presumably to get tankards — when she spoke.

"'Tis nay trouble, Sasha. I am the one tae be sorry, sae overly sorry for Deirdre's clumsiness. I'm guessing 'tis the first time ye hae been muddy since ye were a child. Go on and get yourself cleanit up and put the clean clothes on."

And then Sasha went over to the table and started to put her hands into the pot of broth as if to wash them. It was fresh off the fire, and she cried out in pain, lifting her hands out again quickly as soon as one of them touched the surface. He had seen burns before, on the field of battle. This one on her small finger wasn't terribly bad, but probably still painful.

Just in case the lass had gone mad, he went over and restrained her from putting her hand back in the broth again.

"Eileen, the lass has burned her hand. Hae ye any butter?"

Eileen came tearing around the hearth with a very concerned look on her face and the butter dish in her hands.

"Deirdre? Did ye touch the soup pot, lass?"

The wee lass came running up to the table from her position among the younger children, where she had been shepherding them.

"'Tis na me, Maw. Sasha put her hand in the broth." She turned to the bonnie mad lass. "Why did ye dae it? Dae ye eat broth with yer hands where ye come from?"

Sasha pulled her hand away from the butter that Eileen was trying to rub on her burn. Aye, she had verily gone mad.

"Nay, butter and other oils will only make a burn keep burning, deeper doon into the flesh. Please, just give me some cauld water tae plunge it in, and can ye hurry? Sorry tae hae ruined yer soup." She looked down at Deirdre. "I didna ken it was soup. I had thought it was hot water for washing. Where dae ye wash up?"

Deirdre pulled the wash rag out of the pile of clothing Eileen had given Sasha.

"Maw meant for ye tae rub the mud off o yerself with this. Washing is some aught we dae tae the clothing and the dishes. Ourselves we just clean, with rags like this one. Dae ye wash yer hands where ye live?"

Eileen brought in two tankards of water from her cistern and plunked them down on the table along with a bunch of empty ones, which she began to fill with broth using a ladle.

Sure enough, Sasha plunged her hand into one of the tankards of cold water. Only this time, she sighed in relief.

"Thank ye. This is taking the burn away. Ah. It feels better already. Aye, cauld water is the best thing for burns, even better with some ice in it, but I understand 'tis not likely ye hae ice." She laughed a little, but unlike her marvelous unchained liveliness out in the market with the flute, this was an uncomfortable laugh, born of nervousness and embarrassment. It didn't suit her at all.

But at least she wasn't mad. Just verra limited in her knowledge of the world away from home. Just as Tavish had said. It was becoming clear why the man had been so reluctant to leave her here. She really was in need of looking after. A job he had volunteered for and would gladly fulfill.

"Hold on. I shall go and get ye some ice."

The look of surprise on her face as he left was priceless.

On his way back from the icehouse, he fell in beside his brother Alfred, who was also walking toward Eileen's and gave him a face of pleasant surprise.

"I didna expect tae see ye at dinner this evening. What's the ice for?"

"I didna expect tae be there. The ice is for a burn tae the hand of Sasha, another of Tavish's clanswomen, just arrived today. 'Tis her first time away from the MacGregor lands, and she tried tae wash her hands in the bairns's before-dinner broth."

Alfred puzzled over this the three dozen steps back to Eileen's, making sideways glances at Seumas — clearly in order to discern whether he was pulling his leg or not.

"Yer eyes seem awfully bright for a routine look intae the icehouse. She must be at least as special as Kelsey."

Seumas gave his older brother a half serious stern look, holding it extra long for emphasis.

"Ye just save all yer attention for Eileen, and we wull continue tae get along fine."

At first his blond brother's face was amused, but then it turned concerned, and he stopped in the darkening street a moment, turning to him to make sure his next comment was heeded.

"Watch yer heart, Seumas. But a few days ago, ye were trying tae give it tae Kelsey."

Seumas threw his hand out toward the side as if throwing the thought away.

"Och, I am easily ower that now, believe me."

Alfred chuckled a bit.

"Even sae? How can Tavish's clan hae more than one sae lovely lass? And is this one also old enough to be wise and yet sae untouched by the ravages of time? And yet she has done something sae delightfully silly and childlike as tae wash in the broth?"

As he opened the door, Seumas nodded inside toward the table with an amused 'See what I mean?' look.

Ceithir (4)

The cold water felt heavenly on Sasha's hand while she watched in fascination as the gorgeous blonde Eileen dipped tankards of broth, cooled them a bit with cool water, and handed them to her blond children. Even the youngest child, the little girl toddler Sìle, held her uncovered tankard and sipped from it without spilling a drop, making it look easy. Sìle was dressed just like her mother in miniature, rather than in toddler clothes. This made the sight of her daintily sipping from a tankard all the cuter. Eileen disappeared around the hearth into the kitchen area again for a while and then once the children were finished drinking their broth she came back around, once more covered in flour.

"Aodh and Niall, ye two set the table, aye?"

"Aye!"

"Aye!"

The two miniature men made a game of it, mock sword fighting with the knives and using the wooden plates as shields.

Sasha had to dodge them twice as they came by, even though she was making her presence known with her coaching comments.

"Aodh, his left side is open. Niall, ye need to block better, lad."

She was itching to take a movie. It would be difficult with her hand in a tankard though, so it would have to wait. But she would at least get pictures of these adorable mini adults before she left.

There was a knock at the door, and Deirdre ran over and opened it, then turned her head to yell over her shoulder.

"Maw! Seumas is come with the ice! And he brought yer new man!" She turned back to Seumas. "I'm sae glad ye returned." She made a grand gesture into the house. "Will ye come in?"

Seumas gracefully bowed his head to Deirdre and came over and plopped a small chunk of ice in Sasha's water tankard before he nodded toward a door Sasha hadn't noticed before.

"Sasha, this is my brother Alfred. Now go on intae the bedroom and put on those dry clothes sae we can all eat supper."

After Sasha and Alfred exchanged pleasantries, Deirdre scampered up to Sasha and spoke solemnly.

"May I help ye? I'm verra good at putting on clothes."

Sasha breathed a sigh of relief at this and took her

tankard with her on the way to the door, speaking just as Eileen opened her mouth to reign her daughter in.

"I would be delighted tae hae ye help me, Deirdre. The clothes here are just different enough from where I come from that I dae feel the need for a bit o help."

Understatement of the month. These clothes were riddled with little tie strings, and not a button nor a zipper in sight. Sasha hated to think how long it would've taken her to figure it all out on her own, but with Deirdre's help she was changed in a few minutes.

Eileen had told her to leave her muddy clothes in a pile on the floor and she would wash them, and Sasha hadn't known what to say. She'd always dry cleaned her wool suits, but she couldn't exactly tell Eileen that. And the woman was a weaver, so after an awkward pause she had agreed on the condition that she could help. It wouldn't hurt to find out how to wash wool by hand without it shrinking, now would it?

Eileen was shorter than her, so on Sasha, these skirts didn't quite reach the floor the way they did on Eileen and all the other women who'd been out in the market. But otherwise, the skirted shirt with huge sleeves and the plaid overdress fit well. Fortunately, her long hair hadn't gotten muddy.

Glad that it was the style in this time for women to wear their hair down and long, she got her hairbrush out of her purse, but before she could brush the second stroke, Deirdre was squealing and jumping up and down in excitement. Oops.

"That is the brawest thing I did ever see! May I try?"

With the tiniest bit of trepidation, Sasha handed Deirdre the brush and turned her back to her so that the little girl could brush her hair.

"Sure."

The brushing she got only hurt a little bit and only snagged once. Deirdre was pretty skilled with a brush. It didn't go so well when Sasha brushed her own hair, so she didn't complain. Just closed her eyes and clenched her teeth to bear it.

When it was done and she turned around to take her brush back, Deirdre was gazing at it in awe.

Ack! No wonder. Her hairbrush was made of see-through pink plastic with little silver flecks of glitter inside.

Hm. Her impulse was to give the brush to the little girl as a gift. But something Kelsey had said lingered in the back of Sasha's mind. There was danger here from some Druid named Brian who was locked up in a tower, and maybe there were more Druids about. And they were all dangerous.

All she knew about Druids was that they used the magic of the natural realm — they thought of it as the life force that ran through all living things. And she only knew that from the occasional comments she would overhear during her brother's weekly Dungeons and Dragons games in the basement of their parents' house when she was a kid. Okay, she had hidden at the top of the stairs and cracked the door open and leaned into the crack so that she could overhear as much as possible, the games had been so entertaining. The point was, she didn't really know very much about Druids, only what some game said about them.

But she knew Druids could definitely be dangerous. And they had sent Tavish here, so they knew about time travel and would recognize this as being from the future. And time travel was a big secret, judging by the lengths Tavish and Kelsey were going to in their disguises. Who knew what the Druids might do to poor little Deirdre if they thought she knew their secret?

So Sasha decided on a different gift for Deirdre, and held out her hand to be given the hairbrush back.

"Yer turn."

With a huge pretty smile, Deirdre turned around and fluffed her long blonde hair over her shoulders so that it hung down her back.

Sasha knew that after supper, she was going to need the privy she had seen on her way in, and she was not looking forward to that. Ooh. Except that would give her the chance to get her phone situated someplace where it couldn't be seen but where she could use it to take movies of all these precocious kids.

Excited at the prospect, she finished brushing Deirdre's hair and jumped up, grabbing her hand and taking her into the other room to find Tavish and Kelsey standing just inside the front door, looking around in visible apprehension.

Kelsey relaxed and smiled when she saw Sasha enter the room.

"There ye are, Butterfly! Dinna dae that tae me ever again!"

Sasha smiled and raised her shoulder and gave Kelsey her traditional star wave.

"I willna, dinna fash."

But Tavish gestured out the door impatiently.

"Come now, Sasha —"

Oh no he didn't. Couldn't he see that everyone was just sitting down to supper and there were places set for them? She liked Eileen, and it would be rude to leave right now. She gestured toward two places together.

"Tavish, please."

But instead of moving toward their seats, Tavish agitatedly whispered in Kelsey's ear, plainly trying to get her to make Sasha leave.

Was he crazy? She didn't understand it. Rudeness certainly was not the way to avoid calling attention to yourself.

Apparently Alfred agreed, because the captain stood from his seat and called his guard Tavish on it, gesturing at the two empty seats next to each other lest Tavish overlook them one more second.

"Ye are na going anywhere till ye sit down and eat the food Eileen prepared for ye."

Tavish paused, which could not lead to anything good.

She needed to keep him from starting something ugly. In order to distract everyone's attention from the two of them, Sasha picked that moment to steer Deirdre over to the empty seat between Aodh and Niall.

"Thank ye again for the loan o yer daughter, Eileen. She was a verra big help, even brushed my hair for me, see?" She made a show of turning around and showing off how nicely brushed her long red hair was.

Deirdre glowed with pride, and Eileen smiled at her daughter and caressed her cheek.

Sasha moved herself toward the empty seat between Seumas and Alfred.

Seumas pulled the chair out for her, and when she smiled her thanks at him, he gestured at her new outfit and smiled his approval. This pleased her way more than she thought it should, and to avoid gawking at him like a fool, she looked back over toward Tavish, truly interested in whatever he was going to choose to do.

He and Kelsey were whispering back and forth quite agitatedly, but at least they were taking their seats and no longer in danger of angering Alfred.

Sasha was embarrassed for her friends and had half resolved to distract the group once more when she noticed that no one else was paying them any mind. In fact, she caught quite a few winks and nods and eye rolls on her friends' behalf. Alfred had sat down and was being passed a dish, Eileen was busy cutting up food on Sile's plate, the little boys were pretend sword-fighting with their forks full of food behind Deirdre's back, and Seumas ... was sipping his ale, amusedly observing her over the rim of his tankard.

"How did ye earn yer nickname, Butterfly?"

Grateful for the presence of the social lubricant, she grabbed her own ale and gulped some down. It was surprisingly light, but good.

"Hae ye na heard the saying, social butterfly?"

"I canna say I hae."

She buttered her bread, doing her best to look at him coquettishly over the top of it now and then.

"Och, wull now. Kelsey does think I am a social butterfly, which is a person who flits from one conversation tae the next, never staying quiet."

His eyes twinkled at her as he chuckled and buttered his own bread.

"Wull now, ye are a bit o that, tae be sure. Ye hae only just met Eileen, and already Deirdre is dressing ye and the wee lads follow yer commands like those o a queen."

Thank goodness she hadn't taken a bite of her bread yet, because this made her laugh. She made it as pretty a laugh as she could, letting the sound come out her nose in a high pitch that she had found most men enjoyed.

"Stop it. I was only playing along with their game. In truth, I thought they were gaun'ae run me ower and just was saying things sae they would notice me."

He had taken a bite of his bread while she was speaking, and he chewed it with a knowing look in his eyes. She took the opportunity to eat some of her bread as well, and it was delicious. She'd forgotten how good home-baked bread was. He noticed her enjoyment of the bread and left off talking for a while, eating and taking obvious pleasure in watching her eat.

As she basked in his glowing admiration, she heard other conversations at the table and noticed that Eileen had succeeded in getting Kelsey's attention.

"Sae dae ye and Sasha both hae rooms at the castle now, or will ye take me up on my offer tae stay with me, the two o ye?"

Kelsey took a deep breath and turned to Tavish, and they whispered and grunted and groaned a lot before he answered Eileen.

"Aye, the lasses will be staying with ye, at least this evening and mayhap a fortnight or more, depending on the sort o duty I get. If that is nay trouble?"

Eileen gave Sasha and Kelsey each a friendly smile.

"'Twill be my pleasure to hae the lasses stay."

Sasha wiped her mouth and kept Eileen's eye, nodding toward the bedroom and then admiring her new outfit.

"We hae tac launder my clothes sae I can give ye this back."

Eileen shook her head prettily as she sipped from her tankard.

"Nay, it suits ye. Keep it. We can work on lengthening the skirt. Yer clothing is like tae raise some eyebrows, and I want for ye tae enjoy yerself while yer with us."

Sasha had just eaten breakfast, and so she wasn't very hungry. Curiously, she saw that Tavish and Kelsey were devouring their food.

"Seumas, finish my food if ye want. I'm done."

The large red-haired man happily dug in.

Sasha got up and played some more tunes on her new flute while everyone else finished eating. Each time she finished a song or took a breath, everyone applauded and cheered. Some even whistled, very much like they would in her time. She took this as encouragement to play even livelier tunes, switching from those she'd learned in school to her favorite pop music.

Whenever she caught Kelsey's eye while she was playing with the pop tunes, her friend burst out laughing and hid her mouth behind her napkin. By chance she caught Tavish's eye once, and he gave her a 'told you so' look. At first, she had no idea he was thinking, but then she realized she was dancing sort of jig around the table as she played the music, and it was her turn to burst into laughter.

The dishes got done in record time, with three women and young Deirdre helping. And then they all joined the men and boys around the roaring fire they had built in the center fireplace.

Alfred's smile for Eileen was like the moon and stars when she reentered the room.

"Tavish and Seumas and I will get ye more firewood tomorrow, tae make up for all that we're using this evening."

Eileen sat very close to him, and they cuddled a bit by the fire. Their closeness gave Sasha a warm fuzzy feeling, and she savored it, smiling down at them before she looked around for her own place to sit down.

Seumas gave her a more mischievous smile with an alluring twinkle in his eyes as he patted the seat next to him.

She made a show of looking around for any other place to sit down as she slowly made her way over to him, holding her skirts and moving them from side to side. And then Deirdre rushed over and grabbed her hand, and she had another vision.

Oh no.

Deirdre's lifeless body soaking wet and being pulled out of the water onto the seashore. Her face so white, not even a tinge of pink in those sweet little cheeks.

As before, Sasha tried to remember anything and everything she could from the short time she saw it. But that was it. That was all she could find in the vision. How awful.

When she came back to herself, Seumas was now standing next to her, supporting her by her elbow with his strong hand, with his other hand on her back, while Deirdre was sitting at her mother's lap, looking confused. Eileen stroked her daughter's hair and gave Sasha a worried smile.

Seumas spoke softly near her ear once Sasha met his eyes, which looked more worried about her than curious.

"Dinna tell me this time 'twas but a case of déjà vu, Butterfly."

Abashed, she gave him an apologetic smile.

"I tell ye true, this has never happened tae me afore today, and I thank ye for being here for me both times."

They stood there gazing into each other's eyes. His worry had given way to skepticism and doubt, but the majority of what she saw on his face was admiration for her, and good humor. She did her best to show the admiration she had for him, and the fun she'd been having today.

Someone cleared their throat, and Sasha looked over to see that while Eileen remained seated with her arm around yawning Aodh and holding Sile in her lap, Alfred had stood up.

"We're keeping these bairns from bed tae late, and we men hae duty in the morning." He turned to Eileen, who smiled up at him in a way that let Sasha know the two of them had already discussed his leaving. "So we bid ye all good evening with the hope o doing this again tomorrow."

Seumas took Sasha's hand and squeezed it once, then started walking toward Alfred. Eileen nodded at Alfred and escorted the men to the door among many more pleasantries and a very clingy goodbye between Tavish and Kelsey, with a dozen more whispers.

When the wooden plank door had closed and the men were on the other side, Eileen explained that Sasha and Kelsey would have the children's bed out here and she would take the children into the bedroom with her.

Once all the children had hugged her goodnight and the two of them were safely alone in the room, Sasha whispered to Kelsey.

"So what's the plan?"

But instead of answering her directly, Kelsey rolled over so that her back was to Sasha and said in a falling asleep voice, "It would take way too long to explain. Go to sleep, and once you're dreaming, I'll show you."

Còig (5)

At first, Sasha found it hard to fall asleep. She was in a strange place, to say the least. But her best friend was with her, the pile of blankets on the bed was heavy and comforting, and last but not least, she'd had a very exciting day. Once she allowed herself to relax, sleep came swiftly.

Almost as soon as she succumbed, she found herself with Kelsey in what she knew was a dream, because they were sitting in Eileen's dining chairs in their twenty-first century clothes. Pants felt comforting after a whole day in long skirts with nothing under them. Even the pantyhose she hated would have been better.

Unsure how much time they had, Sasha rushed to speak to her friend.

"Kelsey, I've had the oddest visions lately. When Seumas first touched me, I saw him lying outside wounded, with terrible burns on his shoulder. It was awful. And then after dinner tonight, Deirdre grabbed me and I saw her pulled out of the water sopping wet. She was drowned, Kelsey. Both of these visions have really upset me. I don't know what to make of them, and I know it sounds crazy, but somehow I know my visions are going to come true."

Kelsey didn't seem at all surprised. Hm.

"Sasha, I'm going to tell you a bunch of stuff that seems unrelated, but bear with me, okay?"

"Uh, okay."

"When I first came here to the thirteenth century, Brian the Druid looked at my uni ring and called me Priestess."

"He called you Priestess?"

"Yep."

"Are you sure he wasn't joking?"

"I'm sure. He was not joking. He's not the type who jokes, at least not with women. More like against us."

This sounded bad, especially with the sour expression on Kelsey's face. Sasha took her friend's hand.

"Kelsey, if you need to talk about anything, I'm here for you, anytime. You know that, right?"

Kelsey gently squeezed her hand and let go.

"Thanks. Maybe later, but right now there's a lot of other stuff I need you to understand."

There was more?

"Okay."

"So yeah, Brian called me Priestess, and then later, the elite crew of professors met with me and Tavish

— they'd promised to be in touch, and believe me, they are. They included me in his assignment to get a sword, so I'm pretty sure they feel like they can order me around just like they can order Tavish around."

"Wait a sec. I'm confused. How come they can order Tavish around? He wasn't a student at Celtic."

Kelsey made a face that meant 'I'm an idiot.'

"Right, right, right. Okay. Generations ago, Tavish's ancestor made some kind of deal with the Druids. It's convoluted, but right now all you have to know is because of that deal, he's their slave. Well, and it's their power — their magic — that allows him to time travel. Are you with me so far?"

"Uh, I want to say that's ridiculous, but…" Sasha gestured at the dream-world version of Eileen's house and the two of them sitting in their jeans and T-shirts. "Under the circumstances, yeah, I guess I am with you so far."

"Good. So the reason they make him time travel is to get things for them."

"This is getting good. What kind of things – and why don't the druids just time travel themselves and get these things? Time traveling's fun. You'd think they'd be all over it."

"Last time, the thing we were told to get was a magic scepter. This time, it's a magic sword. And when Tavish uses their ring to time travel, he comes back to our time the instant he left it. No time passes while he's gone. So time travel makes you seem to age faster in your own time. That's why Tavish looks five years older than me. He's been here in Eileen's time for five years these past three months of our time."

"Wow."

"Yeah. So anyway, the druids don't want to age

that fast in their own time, so they pop in now and then, but mostly they make others do the time traveling for them. Mostly. Oh, and when Tavish and I left for our time?"

"Yeah?"

"How long were we gone, from your point of view?"

"Half an hour?"

"Yeah, and that was the time it took us to walk to the end of the middle corridor and back. But we spent two months back in our time—"

"Two months! That's longer than I usually go without calling my mother. She'll be worried."

"Nah, I covered for you."

"What did you say?"

"That you met a guy."

They looked at each other and grinned — Sasha sheepishly and Kelsey teasingly.

"Okay, and my obvious question is why would Tavish give the Druids a magic scepter — but oh yeah, he's their slave. Hm. That kind of sucks. Was it at least a benign magic scepter?"

"I hope so. All I could tell was that it was magic. Curiously, Tavish couldn't tell that. With the sword we're looking for now, the elite crew told me it was magic ahead of time. And that brings me to the other things you need to understand." Kelsey held up her right hand, with her class ring on it. "Brian the Druid called me a priestess when he saw this ring. I'm assuming he meant I'm a Druid priestess. And the Druids Tavish reports to back home are the elite crew of professors at Celtic. They're real Druids who can use real magic – and who have slaves."

"About that last part. Tavish is really a slave? As in

he has to do what they say or they whip him and stuff?"

"No. As in he magically has to do what they say. Period."

"Whoa."

"Yeah."

"Kelsey —"

But her friend held up her hand, indicating she was not going to hear Sasha's advice.

"I know it's not the brightest thing to do, being with someone who's a slave to others. But he's the one for me. End of story. Not going to discuss that."

Sasha felt like she had to try again. This was madness.

"But —"

"Sasha, it's not very smart of you to be flirting with Seumas. It can only lead to one or both of you getting your hearts broken. You'll be going back to our time and living there, right? I mean, I can't see you settling anyplace that doesn't have a hairdryer, much less no running water. I know I'm right, but I want to hear you say it."

Sasha held up her hand the exact same way Kelsey had before.

"Okay. You made your point. I don't want to hear your advice, so I can see how you don't want to hear mine."

Kelsey drew her knees up in front of her, and suddenly her feet were on another chair that hadn't been there a moment ago.

"Yeah. So anyway, perhaps all the professors at our university are Druids, but for sure the elite crew are. And Druids do evil things like enslave people. And at least one Druid from eight hundred years ago thinks we're also Druids because we wear these rings."

"But how can we be Druids? Druids can do magic."

"But we can do magic, Sasha. I can dream walk, and you have second sight."

Kelsey sat there, quietly meeting Sasha's gaze, visibly and patiently waiting for what she had said to sink in.

Sasha's rational mind fought it for the longest time. How ridiculous. But of course finally she had to accept it for the truth, just as she had accepted time travel. At long last she spoke.

"So where's the sword you're supposed to get?"

Kelsey got up, and suddenly Sasha was standing next to her, without having moved.

"I don't know where it is, but I do know someone who probably does. Come on. Tavish and I were going to show you where the tower was anyway. Might as well do it now."

What happened next was one of the weirdest things Sasha ever experienced. She started to walk toward the door, but quick as thought, she and Kelsey were at the castle entrance that she had seen while they walked from the underground exit into the castle town.

Just a dream. Just a dream.

Once she got that settled in her mind, Sasha paused and admired a much larger and more fortified castle than was still here in her time, before entering.

"Seems like a week ago that I saw this entrance as we walked by, but for me, it's only been a few hours."

Kelsey nodded sympathetically.

"And you've only time traveled once. I'm on my

fifth time – been here and back, here and back, and now here again. Dream walking was very weird for me at first too, but two and a half months later, it's almost second nature. Don't try to move." She laughed. "And I'll try to quit suggesting you move. Just stand here with me while I move us around. Pretend you're in Willy Wonka's great glass elevator. You'll get far less disoriented."

Sasha tried it, and as long as she concentrated on just standing there and watching things go by, it worked. They went into a banquet hall first, complete with iron chandeliers. Then down several stone hallways with tapestries on the walls depicting natural scenes and finally up a long stairway that spiraled up a corner tower.

Kelsey paused before they could see the top.

"Now, the reason we were going to show you this before was so that you don't come up this way in real life. It's not very likely that you'd come here by accident, but we wanted to be sure. Do you think you can manage to not find your way up here?" Her friend smiled at how oddly she had phrased that.

Sasha nodded.

"Yeah. I think I've got it mapped out."

Kelsey looked thoughtful for a moment.

"Hm, I'm going to make you invisible, so don't say anything and he won't even know you're with me."

"O-kay."

Kelsey laughed softly.

And then Sasha looked down and saw the stairs where her long skirts should be. Panic surged through her, making her heart race and her breath catch. She gulped in several deep breaths.

Just a dream. Just a dream.

She got ahold of herself just in time to float up the last curve in the stone stairs without being able to see herself. She had to resist the urge to go 'Who-oo-oo-oo' like a ghost.

And then they were up at the top of the stone tower in a dead-end stone hallway with a stone ceiling in front of the tower-room door. It was solid oak and had a little window at face height with three iron bars going up and down.

And with his face to the window, fists holding the iron bars, was a man who could only be Brian the Druid. He wore a white robe and had long white hair.

"Priestess! Ye hae come tae see me."

Kelsey made an oddly shaped bronze sword appear in her hand.

"Brian, tell me where this sword is. Tell me now."

Brian got a look of wonder on his face as he gazed at the sword.

"Galdus?"

Kelsey leaned in toward Brian with visible eagerness.

"Who's Galdus? Is this his sword? Ye ken where it is, do ye nay. Where is it?"

Brian cackled like an old woman.

"Dae tell me what it's like in yer time, Priestess. Surely ye hae an artifact from then ye can trade me for this one oor colleagues o the future hae sent ye back for."

That didn't sound like a good idea. Sasha prayed that Kelsey didn't fall for it.

But she appeared to be considering it.

Brian pressed his advantage.

"Aw, I am na gaun'ae show it tae anybody up here in this tower. I just want tae see it, tae know some aught o the future." His eyes looked eager and kind of deranged. "How dae ye keep yer skin sae smooth and yer hands sae callous free? Does everyone in the future use magic, with nary a need for work? Tell me it is sae!"

Kelsey nodded slowly, and the look on her face was... apologetic. As if it were her fault that he was born in the wrong century and didn't have all our modern conveniences.

"Aye, 'tis now magic, but 'tis true. We hae machines that dae all the hard work for us. They dae the threshing and the sowing and the harvest. They bring us water and heat it for us and take away oor waste. They transport us, even fly us. And they build other machines. It truly is a wonder, and I never appreciatit it until I came back tae now and saw juist how hard life can be for the workers, especially in the fields. But na everyone has all these things. Only aboot one percent o the world does. I'm sae blessed, and I ought tae be more grateful."

Brian's face wore a mixture of enthusiasm and puzzlement.

"How sae, lass? What is a machine?"

Sasha was puzzled too. Kelsey had said this man was dangerous, so why was she trying so hard to explain the future to him? Why did she care?

It wasn't like her friend to not notice when someone was leading her away from the subject she had come to discuss. In this case, the sword. It was very tempting to speak up and ask these questions, but maybe being hidden would turn out to be an advantage, so she remained silent.

Kelsey was uncharacteristically bland and unanimated. As she spoke, she got closer and closer to Brian, until their noses were almost touching.

"A machine is a slave that doesna live, made o materials mined from the yard and powerit by what may and all be magic, I have sae little understanding o how it works."

As she spoke, Brian's arms slithered out of the opening in the door through the bars like snakes, cold and slow.

Sasha's breath caught when she realized what he was going to do.

He looked right at Sasha and winked at her.

She screamed.

Kelsey startled out of whatever trance Brian had put her in. In one continuous movement, she pushed off the door, grabbed Sasha's hand, and blinked them out of the tower and clean back to their own time.

Sasha found herself sitting in a trailer she'd never been in before, but it looked familiar. As she spoke, she offhandedly realized this was the blue on blue interior she and Kelsey had picked out. Mr. Blair had gotten it for them. It was nice.

But far from being idle, their conversation was more of the panicked variety.

"Kelsey, he put you in some kind of trance. I thought you were going to open the door and let him out, you were acting so off. How can he put you in a trance inside of a dream you control?"

Kelsey shuddered and hugged herself.

"Obviously, I'm a lot less powerful a dream walker that I imagined. I knew Brian had the power to put people under a trance. He's made Tavish sleep before. But I had no idea he could do that inside a dream. We're lucky to have gotten away."

Sasha nodded. Noticing that her hands were

shaking, she sat on them.

"You also need to know you were not able to hide me from him. He looked right at me and winked before he tried to grab you. That's what made me scream, it was so creepy."

Kelsey bit her lip and looked all around.

"I hope we're safe from him here. I hope he can't follow us to our time in the dream world."

Sasha shrugged and shook her head.

"If he can do that, then we're screwed. There's no sense in worrying about it. Our bodies are back at Eileen's house asleep. I think we should send our consciousnesses there to take care of them."

Kelsey was looking at Sasha with respect now.

"You're right. I don't know why I thought he would give us an answer. You should know that the reason he's locked up is because he tried to grab me before in a dream. I'm so stupid. I keep wanting to take shortcuts instead of doing actual research and exploring. And those are the things I went to school to learn how to do." She was nearly crying by the end of this.

Sasha took both of Kelsey's hands in hers.

"Hey, hey, hey. None of that now. Very few people would remain logical in a situation such as ours."

Kelsey opened her mouth to argue and then opened her eyes wide and looked at Sasha and burst out laughing. Sasha joined her in laughter, and they squeezed hands and let go.

Kelsey stood up straight once more and spoke with humor.

"You're right. We should go back to our sleeping bodies and keep them company. Who knows what evil things could happen to us if we left them there too long."

Even though what she said was true, it struck both of them so funny that they dissolved in fits of laughter again. Which felt much better than crying.

While they laughed, another woman their age came out of one of the bedrooms, dressed for sleep in an old T-shirt and ratty old sweats. She was in the middle of redoing her long black ponytail, and she opened the fridge with her knee and bent over to sip through a sports bottle straw before she greeted Sasha. Her eyes were bleary, but they were the most beautiful shade of light brown, almost yellow.

"Hi, I'm Amber. You must be Sasha. Guess you'll be wanting your room back, huh."

Kelsey made an 'oops' face and gestured toward one of the bedrooms, and Amber was gone.

"Sorry about that. I must've walked us into her dream somehow. She was Tomas's girlfriend back when we all hung out together at the faire —"

Sasha held up her hand to stop Kelsey's story.

"Tell me later. Let's get back to Eileen's."

Although Kelsey had been right in what she told Brian about how easy life was in the modern world, Sasha thought there were charms to the old world. She couldn't wait to get back to it, finish sleeping for the night, and wake up there. And seeing Seumas again was only...

Well, let's be honest. Seeing Seumas again was nine tenths of why she was so anxious to get back. She really shouldn't dote too much on him. Kelsey was right. There was no way she could live in the past with him. She could enjoy looking at him in the meantime though, right?

Sia (6)

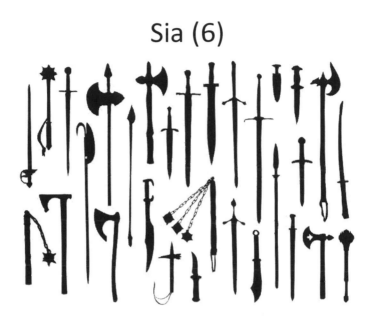

Seumas, Tavish, and Alfred left Eileen's house
together: Alfred headed toward his rooms in the
castle, Seumas and Tavish to the barracks. It was dead
night, but there was plenty of light from the moon.
All the shops were closed except for the two taverns.
Light and raucous laughter spilled out of those.
Seumas felt sure Tavish would approve of him as a
mate for his clanswoman Sasha. The man had come
to the castle town six months ago — a complete
stranger in need of work and lodging — and Seumas
had taken a chance on him when no one else would.
And come to think of it, the man's appearance had

been under suspicious conditions. How could he have forgotten about that?

~*~

Seumas was walking out along the underground tunnel from duty at the stone docks below when he found a stranger wandering around looking at the patterned carvings in the walls as if they were fascinating — which he supposed they were.

As soon as the man saw him, he planted a grateful look on his face.

"How blessed I am that ye came along. Can ye help me out? I'm lost, ye see."

Seumas looked up and down the tunnel. The only way in here that wasn't tightly guarded required crawling up through a narrow passageway that started under the sea, and the man was bone dry. Couldn't have been in here wandering around long enough to dry off, could he?

Best to be direct. And put a little fear in the man. He was much too carefree.

Seamus scowled at him.

"How did ye get doon here?"

The man shook his head and made a funny face that vaguely resembled bafflement but was too dramatic by far. Was he a player? Rare for one of those to be found alone without his troupe.

"I was exploring the caves ootside and I just wanderit in here. Now I canna find ma way oot."

Seumas started walking toward the nearest exit, and the man fell in alongside him. He wasn't sure yet what he was going to do with the man — take him to his uncle for questioning, most likely. If he was a player and had a troupe nearby, that would be a treat.

"I canna see any way ye could hae come in here

withoot us knowing. All o the ways in are guarded. Are ye sure that's what happened?"

The man smiled at him. Smiled. And looked smug.

"Aye. Na all o the ways in are guarded."

"Nay?"

"Nay."

They were at the guard post now, and it was the custom to introduce whoever you were walking with, if they were a stranger. Seumas turned toward the man.

"Tell Dubh and Luthais yer name."

The man bowed at them theatrically, which neither of them had probably ever seen. Seumas only knew it was a theatrical bow because he'd seen a traveling troupe of players while he was being fostered up at Turnberry Castle in Ayrshire. Aye, he was definitely a player, or at least had been, in his younger days. He was going on thirty. Bit old to be traveling alone.

"Tavish McGregor, at yer service."

Dubh and Luthais looked to Seumas, and he shook his head sternly. They moved to seize Tavish, but Seumas held his hand up.

"Tavish says he wanderit intae oor tunnels from an unguarded way in." He looked the man in the face. "Ye had best show me where that is."

Seumas expected Tavish to flinch at that demand, but he rubbed his hands together and smiled at them all as if this were some festival game.

"We wull need a hundred feet o rope."

What? Was Tavish procrastinating in order to put off his doom? But curiosity seized Seumas. And let's face it, the man's enthusiasm was contagious.

Seumas gave Dubh and Luthais a wry grin.

"If there be a landward use for a hundrit feet o

71

rope, then I want tae know what it is. Call for it, Luthais."

The guard whistled, and Cormac came running from the castle with his hand on his sword, eyeing Tavish.

"Aye?"

Seumas kept his eye on Tavish while the other guards explained what they needed.

After a while, Cormac came running back with the rope, and Seumas took him along for good measure. He thought he was a match for Tavish, and the man wasn't armed, but you could never be too sure.

Tavish led them in what seemed a merry chase along the rim of the sea cliff north of the castle.

"Ye dinna guard along here, for ye dinna know. But I will show ye."

He kept looking all around as if for landmarks, both off to the right up high in the mountains and down over the cliff once he'd edged close enough to peer over without falling. At last, he settled near a large stone.

"We did secure the rope tae a ... horse when I went doon last evening. He's gone now, along with Gus the rider, sae let us secure the rope tae this stone."

Cormac looked to Seumas before doing as Tavish said.

Seumas studied Tavish for a moment. The man looked earnest — and not at all addled in the brain — so he nodded for Cormac to go ahead and secure the rope to the stone.

Once it was done, Tavish took the rope and looked to be trying to drag the stone over the cliff. When it wouldn't go, he nodded and walked backward over the edge of the cliff, with only the rope to secure his safety.

Seumas and Cormac ran to the edge of the cliff, sure that when they looked over they would see Tavish dashed on the rocks. Instead, they saw him smiling up at them, his feet against the cliff and walking down it backward, hunched over and holding the rope.

He addressed them with a challenging grin on his face.

"This is callit repelling, where I come from. My hidden way in is nay tae far doon. Here it is. I'll go in and wait for ye."

And with that, Tavish disappeared inside the cliff.

Seumas swore.

Who knew where the man would go now. Nodding to Cormac to hold the rope at the stone against Seumas's greater weight, he took hold of it and backed up over the cliff the same way Tavish had.

By the time they got to his uncle later that day, they were laughing and joking about how Seumas's face had looked when he swung into the hidden way in. Tavish had shown him an imitation of it often enough that it would never leave his mind.

Laird Malcomb had not been as amused as they were.

"The two o ye must secure this hidden way in. Carry rocks down through the tunnels and plug it up."

~*~

Seumas fought the urge to laugh, walking back to the barracks that evening. Talk about a grueling month of labor.

But it had paid off for both of them. Tavish had

turned out to be an excellent guard, even accompanying Seumas on the seaward part of his duty. And Seumas had gotten Tavish accepted by his uncle, and assigned honorable duties.

So Seumas felt sure Tavish would approve of him.

"I tell ye true, Tavish. Sasha draws me. Enough that I could be her husband and be happy all my days. Howsoever, I dinna hae ought tae offer her here, being but the younger son o the laird's sister. Dae ye think yer clan would let me come and join them?"

Tavish looked down at the ground as they walked, rather than look Seumas in the eye. He was definitely keeping a secret. A big one. Why? He had nothing to fear from Seumas. He'd been a stalwart companion.

"I dinna think ye ought to rely on that, Seumas."

Seumas looked to Alfred for support and got a sympathetic look and a shrug.

"I would swear an oath tae yer clan chief and leave my laird behind, ye ken."

Alfred raised his eyebrows at Seumas for that, but said nothing.

Tavish kicked a small rock, and it went skittering away down the street. And then he sighed and turned toward Seumas with a look of great regret. He moved to put a hand on Seumas's shoulder but apparently thought better of it at the last moment, instead gesturing theatrically.

"Would that I could take ye home with me, Seumas. 'Tis not a question o loyalty. That is na the trouble with joining my clan. We're ..." He blinked and turned his head abruptly toward Seumas in a manner that told Seumas he had thought of something unrelated to bring up, allowing him to evade the question. "Ye ken we MacGregors dinna yet hae our own lands, aye?"

Seumas turned to Alfred, whose look was as puzzled as Seumas felt.

"I dinna ken much aboot yer clan at all. Who was Gregor? When did he live?"

Tavish was on the verge of answering the question with pride. Seumas could tell. But the man clammed up and closed his eyes tightly, turning away from him.

They were at the castle gate, and Alfred showed his nonpartisanship in their discussion when he turned his back on them as he walked toward the castle entrance with a toss of his head and a backward wave of his hand.

"See ye in the lists tomorrow."

Seumas waved his brother off with an upward nod, then spoke to Tavish without looking at him. Direct was best.

"I can sense there is a great secret ye keep close tae yer chest. Ye can tell me."

Tavish sighed heavily and threw one of the little stones he'd picked up, knocking some fruit from a tree in the castle garden.

"I wish that I could, Seumas, but nay, I canna."

Seumas stepped up alongside Tavish and rested his forearms on the low castle wall so he could look out into the castle garden as well.

"When ye first came here, I didna trust ye. It wouldna hae been wise for me tae. But with all we hae been through these past five years, now I dae. Dinna ye trust me? Havena I been a friend tae ye?"

Tavish nodded but didn't say anything, and they walked the rest of the way in silence.

Once they were in their racks, Tavish spoke so casually that Seumas knew this was important to him.

"Dae ye ken the story o a sword all encircled, made by a king, wielded by a child?"

Well, two could hold things back, refusing to answer questions. Seumas rolled over on his other side and grunted noncommittally.

What could Tavish possibly feel the need to keep from him? Was the man an outlaw? Nay, he didn't seem so. And Laird Malcomb would've heard something by now, a description of the man, and a warning. Was the man a foreigner? Maybe. He spoke Gaelic very well, but his accent was a little off. He also didn't seem up on the current political climate, but not everyone was a laird's nephew. Anyway, being a foreigner wasn't a crime. It wasn't something that needed to be hidden. So that probably wasn't it.

But Tavish was hiding something. He had all but admitted it, and the man's evasiveness was deeply disturbing. Insulting, even. And worry about this secrecy kept Seumas awake a long time before he finally fell asleep.

~*~

Guard duty with Tavish was strained all the next day, starting bright and early. The two of them were stationed at the stone docks at the bottom of the underground tunnels. The docks had been the site of a battle just a few days before, and tensions were high.

Seumas didn't press his questions. The man had said no, and that needed to be respected.

But the evening lists inside the castle courtyard were a perfect opportunity for Seumas to work out his frustration. They were using wooden practice swords, so the injuries wouldn't be fatal.

"Yer a madman today, Seumas!"

"Look oot, Seumas does mean business."

"Och Seumas, ye can try tae take my leg off, but I'd sooner ye did it with a metal sword."

He showed off, winning all seven of his bouts so far. But after each one, he helped the other man up and the two clasped the forearms of their sword hands in trust and friendship.

And then he and Tavish happened to be next to each other waiting in line for their next bout behind Cormac, who addressed them both.

"I did hear ye last evening, Tavish, asking about the sword all encircled, made by a King, wielded by a child."

"Aye? What can ye tell me aboot it?" Tavish asked him.

"I hae heard the story."

"Aye?" Tavish's interest was definitely piqued.

"Aye. It goes that in the time o our great, great, great granddas, Robert the Bruce was fostered here as a child, and the smithy helped him make a toy sword."

Osgar, the man in front of Cormac in line, nodded.

"I did hear the same tale, howsoever I was told Robert the Bruce was visiting here, nay fostered."

Rob, the man in front of him, shook his head and waved his hand.

"Nay. I'm namit after Robert the Bruce, ye ken? He was fostered here, but he didna make the sword. The smithy made it for him, as a gift."

Behind them, Pòl spoke over the last half of this.

"The way I did hear it, the faeries brought the sword tae the young Bruce as a gift, in exchange for his promise o loyalty in keeping their waurld safe later on in his life."

Warrick had just finished his bout and only heard this last version when he came over and joined the line at the end, which had bent double so as to be close to the conversation. He rushed the end of the line even closer, face red with conviction.

"Yer wrong! How can the sword be made by a king if the faeries hae brought it?"

Pòl got right up into Warrick's face.

"The king o the faeries made it, ye bletherer!"

Seumas put his arms around Warrick and Pòl's shoulders and squeezed them both until they looked away from each other and at him.

"All o yer stories differ a bit from the way I heard it told. Howsoever, it happened long ago, ye ken. And a good story changes each time someone does tell it."

The two backed down, but speculation on the story only ended when they had all separated into their bouts.

And then when Tavish's bout was over, instead of getting in the line again, he passed between the two carts for the practice swords, ducked low to be hidden behind them, and snuck out of the courtyard.

Seumas immediately flubbed his bout and did the same, running once he was in the street to catch up with Tavish in the failing sunlight.

No surprise really. The man was headed toward Eileen's house.

Seumas kept back far enough so as not to be noticed, stooping down below a vendor cart the one time Tavish did stop and look behind him. He remained there, where he had a good vantage of Eileen's front door if he looked through the linen the vendor had draped over everything. He noted in passing that it wasn't nearly so fine as the linen Eileen made.

Sasha was outside, playing a game of stones with Eileen's children. Tavish ran right up to her and grabbed her hand, and she swooned and she was wont to do. Tavish caught her, muttering something about having to take her back.

What could it mean? Wasn't Tavish with Kelsey? Was he greedy enough to want them both? If that was his secret, then he was going to be disappointed. Sasha wasn't interested in Tavish. It could be told by the way she didn't respond when the man held her.

She recovered from her swoon and said something too soft for Seumas to hear. The two of them looked all around suspiciously, called the children, and went inside the house.

Seumas walked up to the door and hung back a bit, looking through the window. He'd give Sasha another chance to respond to Tavish, but if she didn't this time, then he was going to continue his pursuit of her.

But their conversation was the last thing he expected.

"I had anoother vision, just now. Ye and Kelsey were in a different castle, and Kelsey was holding a sword."

Seumas was so engaged with listening to her that he didn't hear Kelsey and Eileen coming up behind him with their shopping baskets until Kelsey spoke to him.

"Dae ye want tae open the door for us, or are ye gaun'ae stay oot here looking in through the window?"

Seachd (7)

Sasha ran across the dirt street to grab the stone that had skipped over there and then threw it to hit the stone she was aiming at. She hit it! She raised her hands up in the air and went dancing all around the group of children, mostly oblivious to the smirks of neighbors looking out their glassless windows to see what the fuss was about.

"Score!"

Sìle sat there sucking her thumb as usual, but Aodh and Niall laughed from their places near the rocks they were aiming at.

Deirdre put her hands on her hips and scolded

them with her index finger and a curl of her lip.

"Ye should na make fun o her. Just because she's not from aroond here and uses funny words does na mean she has nay feelings."

Sasha hugged the little girl to her hip.

"I dinna mind their laughter. 'Tis all in fun."

Eileen's children were delightful, especially Little Deirdre. Her mother probably thought her precocious and slightly annoying sometimes, but Sasha was grateful for all the help the little girl provided. And she would add 'perceptive' to the long list of adjectives her mother doubtless used to describe the wee lass. She was pretty sure Deirdre knew just how clueless and inept Sasha felt here — though certainly not why — and the little six-year-old was such a sweetie to reach out and assist.

Deirdre had been a godsend this morning at the weaver shop, helping Sasha accept Eileen's help cleaning her suit. It was just that the suit had cost her almost a thousand dollars, and she had been cautioned to only dry clean it, lest it shrink.

~*~

Sasha carried her suit close to her chest all the way to Eileen and Kelsey's work. They all walked together in the pre-dawn light, the children too, with Eileen carrying Sile. The door was open when they got there, and two men were already busy on looms.

"Did ye bring us anoother apprentice?"

Kelsey went over to the far right corner of the room and picked up some stuff and started working with it.

"This is my... clanswoman Sasha. These are the other master weavers in toon, Fergus and Uilleam."

The men waved at Sasha, and she waved back,

giving them her friendly smile.

Eileen put the toddler down behind a row of tall buckets on the floor and reached out toward Sasha. No, toward the suit.

Sasha heard Deirdre's voice at her elbow.

"'Tis all right. Maw won't ruin yer clothes. She's a weaver. She knows what she does."

Sasha looked down at the cute little girl.

"Why dae ye say that?"

Deirdre pointed.

"Because ye are hugging yer clothes."

She was. Walking over to Eileen, she forced herself to relax and let out a little laugh before she handed over the suit with a great deal of trepidation. And then she looked down into the buckets.

"Oh. But that's…"

Eileen turned Sasha's suit over in her hands, admiring the workmanship … and probably the machine sewing. Too polite to say anything, she slowly pushed the muddy designer garments into one of the buckets filled with sudsy water, then turned and went over to where Kelsey was, smiling and beckoning for Sasha to join them.

Sasha sank down into a crouch, looking at her submerged suit and all the other submerged clothing in the buckets.

Deirdre hugged her and whispered in her ear.

"Ye dinna hae master weavers where ye live, I ken. Aye, those are kilts. And we make them from wool, like yer clothes. They wash oot fine if ye just sink them slowly and let them be. Go on over and talk with yer friends now. I wull watch the baby."

~*~

It was Sasha's turn again, in the street with the

children. She took careful aim, threw, and missed her target this time.

"Darn!"

The boys were scrunching their noses at her, visibly trying to place that word, when Tavish ran up and grabbed her hand, trying to tug her into the house.

"We hae a lead on the relic we need tae find. Let's take ye back first, and then Kelsey and I'll go. Ye hae already missed tae much time at home, on account o not coming with us when we telt ye tae."

But Sasha wasn't paying attention to what he said. Because she was having another vision.

Tavish and Kelsey wandered a large fortified stone castle. Not the one here. This one had an obvious way to sail a boat right inside it on the water and dock there — Turnberry Castle in Ayrshire, about fifty miles north of here. Now Tavish was looking at Kelsey in wonder, and Kelsey was holding a sword.

Sasha tried to look closer and see if it was the same sword that Kelsey had made appear in front of Brian the Druid, but the vision abruptly ended.

When she came back to herself, Sasha realized she'd swooned again and Tavish had caught her, because he was still holding her. She recovered herself and gave him an awkward smile of thanks.

Still holding her by the hand, he tugged her toward

the door of the house. Just like Kelsey, he wasn't even aware of the children.

She'd been left in charge of them, and although it was probably safe to leave them alone outside here, she just couldn't bring herself to do that.

"Come on in, bairns."

Much to her surprise, there was no groaning or saying 'Do we have to?' They all picked up their favorite stones and ran right inside. She gave them her best smile in gratitude.

"Deirdre, will ye please help by supervising the bairns in setting the table for supper?"

Deirdre just about curtsied in front of her before rushing off to do just that.

Sasha was smiling when she turned to Tavish, but his face was so concerned that she rushed into her explanation of what just happened.

"I had anoother vision, just now. Ye and Kelsey were in a different castle, and Kelsey was holding a sword."

Tavish was about to answer when the door opened and Kelsey and Eileen came in with their shopping baskets, followed closely by Seumas.

Sasha didn't mean to stare, but she couldn't help it. Her gaze landed on him and she just couldn't tear her eyes away. Fortunately, he seemed to be having the same trouble. They smiled at each other in mutual amusement. She was vaguely aware of her surroundings, but mostly she smiled at Seumas and reveled in the fact that he smiled back — and not a tentative 'maybe we're attracted to each other' smile this time. Nope. This was a full blown 'Okay, we're both attracted. Now what?'

Kelsey followed Eileen into the kitchen and

plunked her basket down on the counter. Tavish followed her in there and took her in his arms, dancing with her while holding her in front of him, still looking toward the counter. And doubtless whispering in her ear about the lead he had on the sword they were looking for.

Sasha froze.

He would also tell Kelsey his plan to take her home before they went looking for the sword. And she wasn't ready to go home yet.

Still smiling at Seumas, she spoke aloud to Kelsey in the kitchen from out in the front room.

"I did hae another vision, Kelsey, aboot ye and Tavish at Turnberry Castle in Ayrshire, holding a sword. I didna get a close look at the sword, sae I dinna ken if 'tis the one. Howsoever, it seems like some aught tae go on, aye?"

Seumas raised his eyebrows at her and deepened his smile while also raising his voice so loud that it summoned the children over.

"Aye? All the talk in the lists today was aboot Robert the Bruce as a wee lad, forging a sword right here where we hae the honor o being his foster place..." He went on in detail.

The wee lads in the room were enraptured by the story. They had apparently heard it many times before — which wasn't really surprising, seeing how it had happened right here in their home town. The two of them pantomimed to match the words they spoke along with Seumas in a singsong voice, completing each other's sentences while their sisters looked on and nodded.

Niall made a big circle with his tiny arms.

"A sword all encircled."

Aodh made an imaginary crown on his head with his hands.

"Made by a king."

Niall pretended to have a Claymore in his hands as he swung it with wroth force in an arc that would've removed his brother's head.

"Wielded by a child."

Aodh ducked, and then the two of them were running around the room pretend sword-fighting again.

Seumas raised his eyebrows at Sasha. His eyes were still warm, but puzzled.

"And Robert the Bruce was born at Turnberry Castle. How dae ye ken that was the castle ye saw? Ye canna hae been there, can ye?"

Darn. She had slipped up and shown too much knowledge. How ironic that it was a structure of this time she'd said too much about, rather than an anachronism such as one of the bridges that now joined Scotland's smaller islands to the mainland. She needed to guard her tongue better, to think carefully before each time she spoke.

Tavish and Kelsey came into the room. Tavish did not look happy with Sasha for bringing up her vision in front of everyone. Kelsey looked amused. Even Eileen came in, wiping her hands on a dishtowel.

Sasha put her hands on her hips in a fair imitation of Deirdre and addressed Seumas. She vaguely sensed herself twisting from right to left and back again, making her long skirts sway around her legs. Was this how women flirted back in this day? It frightened her a bit, how easily it came to her. Women's intuition, she guessed.

"Nay, o course I havena been there. The name was

part o the vision. 'Tis a remarkable place, Turnberry Castle, aye? Hae ye been there?"

Her flirting worked. The puzzlement left his eyes, and he was back to twinkling them at her, darn him. He was spoiling her for other men. She was going to miss his attention when she went home. None of the men there knew how to be so attentive.

Seumas nodded and pursed his lips, visibly trying to look smug that he was so important, but Sasha could tell that really he just didn't want her to leave just yet, because he assisted her in turning this into a big deal.

Gazing around at the whole crowd as if they had gathered just to hear his story, he put his foot up on the mantle, posing like an orator.

"Aye, I hae been there, tae Turnberry Castle in Ayrshire. 'Tis much closer tae the water than Laird Malcomb's castle here. Ye can sail yer boat right intae it. There are na caves like we hae here. Nay, instead, the built-up part o the castle comes oot o the water and encircles the docks. They must hae built it all during low tide ower several years."

He bent over to the children's height and looked in each of their faces by turn.

"Either that, or they usit the mermaids."

Aodh and Niall and Sile all giggled at this.

But Deirdre put her hands on her hips again and shook her little finger in Seumas's face.

"There isna such thing as mermaids. Ye should na tell these children fibs like that. They'll grow up nay knowing lies from what is real."

Tavish and Kelsey laughed at that, but Deirdre didn't seem to realize they were laughing at her precociousness. She bent over at the middle and scrunched her eyebrows at them in a lecturing pose.

"I'm serious, ye ken. This is serious business. Raising children is an important task. Ye need to take it seriously."

Each time she said the word 'serious', she jerked her head and stomped her little foot in a manner that was so funny that Tavish and Kelsey burst out laughing again. Eileen was biting her knuckle to keep from laughing, and to her credit, she looked away to hopefully avoid her daughter seeing how amused she was.

Sasha felt bad for Deirdre. The poor little six year-old had a lot of responsibility, watching her younger brothers and sister while her mother worked. Sasha looked at Seumas to see his reaction, and he looked sad for Deirdre too. This warmed her heart.

She turned to Deirdre to try and offer her some comfort.

But the little girl was already huffing off into the bedroom. She slammed the door.

Sasha started to go after Deirdre, but Eileen shook her head no. Sasha honored the mother's wishes, though it made her sad. She silently vowed never again to feel sorry for herself for having a boring childhood. Boring was much better than no childhood. She didn't blame Eileen, though. These were tough times, and Eileen was just raising her children as best she knew how.

Now that Sasha was thinking about it, she noticed there weren't any toys in the house. The children played with stones or with the table settings or with their mother's clothes. Ordinary things and imagination gave them all the fun they were going to have. Oddly, they didn't seem deprived.

Eileen moved back into the kitchen and resumed preparing dinner.

"Aodh, Niall, and Sìle — go intae the bedroom and keep yer sister company while we grown-ups hae a talk oot here, please."

Sasha was again amazed when the children obeyed immediately and without arguing.

Once the adults were alone, Eileen turned to call the rest of them into the kitchen with her, but they'd already come. Kelsey started helping cut vegetables.

Sasha went up to Eileen's other side.

"What manner o help dae ye need?"

Eileen filled a pot up with water from her cistern and set it on the kitchen side of the mantle.

"Ye can gather all the scraps o meat from the larder there and put them in this pot along with the vegetables we cut up, then put the pot on the fire and stir it." She went and got a wooden spoon and handed it to Sasha.

Alfred had arrived in the middle of this and let himself in, and on their own, the men had already started adding wood to the fire and banking the coals so that Sasha could put the pot on them.

Seumas sought Sasha's eyes from across the room and spoke out loud, including Tavish and Kelsey when he did.

"Sae why all the interest in Robert the Bruce and his wee childhood sword?"

With much amusement, Sasha looked to Kelsey to explain this, however she would.

Kelsey put a fake smile on her face and shook with fake excitement, looking askance at Sasha every now and then and probably unaware she was wringing her hands.

"'Tis a favorite story in Sasha's family, and her aged grandmother askit us tae follow up on it tae see which parts are true while she was oot this way, ye ken. And now she's having visions o it. 'Tis quite exciting, aye? I take this as a sign that we need tae go and see." She looked at Sasha to verify her story.

Sasha smiled and nodded, playing along by trying to look a little embarrassed at how much fuss was being made on her behalf.

Tavish gave a huge dramatic nod as if he had just decided they really needed to follow up on this after all. He looked to Alfred with a question in his eyes.

"We dinna hae anything planned ower the next few weeks. Can ye spare me tae go with my clanswomen on this errand, tae keep them safe? I'm thinking Donall can take us there on his way tae Norway, and we can find someone coming back this way once we arrive, so we wull only be gone two weeks at the most."

Before Alfred could answer, Seumas butted in, speaking directly to his brother.

"If Sasha and Kelsey go on this errand, then I insist on going along. I hae been tae Turnberry afore and can act as a guide."

Visibly amused, Alfred looked from one man to the other and then over at Kelsey and Sasha before he shared a wink with Eileen.

"Hoo aboot it, Eileen? Kelsey and Sasha are yer apprentices. Can ye spare them from the weaver shop for as much as two weeks?"

Eileen scrunched her nose and shrugged as she dumped the rest of the vegetables into the pot and helped Sasha put it on the coals of the fire.

"I dinna ken."

Seumas knew Eileen was teasing and meant to wait her out. Sasha could tell because of the way his eyes twinkled and his lips pursed together.

Tavish, on the other hand, looked like he was about to lay down the law and reclaim his clanswomen from their apprenticeship.

Fortunately, Kelsey jumped in.

"How about if we bring you presents from Ayrshire, Eileen?"

Eileen smiled really big and looked around at her house.

"Ooh! What manner o presents dae ye propose tae bring?"

Kelsey shrugged.

"I dinna ken, now having been to the place. Howsoever, we wull bring ye some ought that ye wull treasure. Ye hae my word upon it."

Eileen came over and gave Kelsey a hug, and then pulled Sasha over and hugged her as well.

"Ye are women after my own heart, sae I suppose ye can go."

They laughed and talked the rest of the evening about the legend of Robert the Bruce's childhood sword and the voyage to the castle and what manner of presents Eileen would get.

Captain Donnell was scheduled to leave the next day, so they resolved to be up at dawn and head down to Port Patrick to ask him for passage.

Eileen brought out some wine she'd been saving for a special occasion, and they all merrily toasted.

"Bon voyage."

Sasha and Kelsey were in good spirits as they got into bed for the night. Just as they blew out the candle, she caught sight of Deirdre looking at her intently. But when Sasha opened her mouth to say something, the little girl looked away and quickly went into the bedroom and closed the door.

Ochd (8)

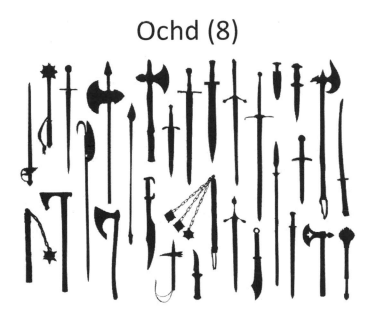

Seumas knew that he and Tavish were getting a special favor from Alfred because he was his brother. No one else would be allowed to go on a trip just because someone's grandmother had heard a story. Normally, he would feel guilty for getting special treatment that none of the other guards got to have, but today he had a huge smile on his face as he and Tavish walked down to Eileen's from the barracks. Tavish knocked on Eileen's door, and Kelsey let them in.

"We're ready tae go," she whispered. "Eileen and the children are still asleep. We didna hae much tae pack, but she insistit we take these provisions for the trip." She held up a knapsack.

Sasha came to the door then. She was wearing the clothes Eileen had loaned her — proper long skirts that didn't show her boots — and she clutched Tavish's plaid cloak around her tightly against the morning cold. She had braided her hair against the sea breeze, the same as he.

He got out the knife and held it out to her.

"Here. My da gave this tae me when I was a child. 'Tis now longer large enough, ye ken. But 'tis the proper size for ye. Put it in yer belt. Ye at least need tae hae a knife."

She took it from him as she and Kelsey came out the door, then intently stared at it for a few moments before giving him a huge smile that lit up her whole face and made her beauty shine like the rays of the sun rising over the distant mountains. She fell into step beside him as they walked along the cliff path to Port Patrick with the sea on their left, fiddling with the knife and her belt as if she'd never belted a knife before.

"Thank ye. 'Tis such a fine gift. I wull treasure it always."

Hm. It was fun having this effect on a woman. It had been a long time, and nothing much had come of it before. Here was hoping for this time.

He gently took the knife from her hand and secured it through her belt, conscious of the smoothness of her hand when it released the knife and the warmth of her middle when his fingers brushed against her dress in order to belt it.

He turned around and walked backward in front of her, admiring his handiwork.

"Now ye are ready for a journey."

She laughed, humoring him. When they got to the cliff side with the view down to the right into Port Patrick, she froze and stared down there in apparent awe. He followed her gaze and looked down with a mind to see it as a newcomer would. Someone who had never left their home... Oh.

She started walking again, but she was still looking down into the port.

"The ships are sae beautiful. I had heard aboot them and seen... drawings, but tae see them in front o me? It is stunning."

He took her right hand and placed it firmly on his raised left arm, putting his right hand over hers so that she couldn't withdraw it.

"Go on and gander, lass. Howsoever, the last thing I dae need is for ye tae fall."

It might've been his imagination, but he thought for a moment she squeezed his forearm.

They amicably walked arm in arm without talking to each other for the rest of the way to Captain Donnell's ship, listening to Kelsey and Tavish speculate on whether they'd actually find Robert the Bruce's sword or just more stories.

But Captain Donnell's apologetic face told Seumas right away that he didn't have room for them.

"Sorry lads. Howsoever, ye can see I'm near the waterline already, with all o the cargo I'm carrying for Norway. Ye might ask Captain Dowd does he hae room for the four o ye." He gestured over toward another ship that was loading and then lowered his voice to almost a whisper. "Mind ye though, he is na verra likable."

Kelsey laughed inappropriately at this, and

Seumas's breath caught in his throat.

Aye, it was true that Captain Donnell wasn't very likable himself, but you didn't laugh at a captain. Fortunately she had impressed the captain and made him a fair bit of extra money a few days ago, and he let it slide.

Seumas looked over at Sasha to see if she was aware of her clanswoman's faux pas. Good. She was more socially graceful than the other woman, though they both seemed highborn. Far be it from him to entertain snobbery about another's lack of grace, but he would only be able to kill so many men in defense of his woman before even being the nephew of the local Laird wouldn't secure his position here.

Letting out his breath and relaxing a bit, Seumas looked to Tavish, who nodded a bit grimly that yes, he still wanted to go, even if they couldn't go with Captain Donnell.

So Seumas addressed the captain.

"Aye, we wull go with Captain Dowd."

At this, Donnell waved until someone on Dowd's ship noticed and then gestured that the four of them were coming over.

Captain Dowd's ship wasn't as in good a trim as Captain Donnell's, but she looked seaworthy. Oh, it was this man. Seumas had seen him around Castleton a few times, always arguing with the local tradesmen. Well, it was a short journey to Turnberry Castle, not even half the day by ship. They could abide.

A look at Tavish told him he was thinking the same thing. How could his friend be so easygoing about most things, and yet keep some huge secret from a man whose life he had saved and who had saved his? Well, Seumas wasn't going to let it get to him.

He was holding Sasha's arm to help her aboard when the captain approached them with his nose in the air and a sneer on his freckled face.

"Oh we hae Laird Malcomb's nephew himself, eh? Not enough room for ye on yer preferred ship, sae I take it. Wull ye willna be leisurely passengers, ye ken. Ye wull have tae work." He looked Sasha and Kelsey over with just enough good manners that Seumas didn't cut him down on the spot. But it was close. "I suppose yer lasses can sit that oot." He caught the attention of one of his crewmembers and then pointed at Tavish and Seumas. "Get these two tae work loading the cargo."

Seumas found Sasha and Kelsey a seat in the bow of the boat, where they would be out of the way. He took Sasha's hand in his, but included Kelsey in what he had to say.

"I hae noticed that the two o ye feel free tae take a lot o liberty in yer actions. That is good for ye in yer own village and even here when amoong friends. I would na take it away from ye. Howsoever, while yer on Captain Dowd's ship, ye must dae what he says, ye ken?"

Sasha smiled at him with understanding. Kelsey at least gave a grudging nod.

Tavish was already working, and Seumas gave Sasha's hand a gentle caress before he let go and went off to join him. They loaded all manner of goods into the ship from all over the world: spices from India, tea from China, rugs from Persia… Captain Dowd worked for a wealthy man, indeed.

Finally, all the cargo was loaded and it was time to cast off — and for Seumas and Tavish to go check on the lasses. He heard Sasha's distress before he saw her, and when he did, her face was green.

Kelsey tried to chase him off.

"Seumas, why dinna ye and Tavish go talk tae the men o the ship? Ask them if they hae ever heard the story o Robert the Bruce's sword and if they think it's at Turnberry Castle?"

Tavish moved to Kelsey's side and held her close, making it look like affection when really Seumas knew it was protectiveness — and a determination not to let her separate herself from him and get in trouble here among men who didn't often see lasses up close and so personal.

So Seumas addressed her, but really he was talking to Tavish.

"Go on and enjoy the sights, Kelsey. I ken the way o the sea, sae I can help Sasha with her grumbly stomach."

Kelsey looked to Sasha, who subtly nodded her head astern. Heh!

Once Tavish and Kelsey had walked away and down into the hold leaving him relatively alone with Sasha, he made it his mission to distract her. Standing behind her with them both facing the bow as the ship got unsteadily underway, he leaned in close to her cheek and whispered, pointing.

"Dae ye see off in the distance there?" He pointed off to the right where the cliffs opposite those they'd arrived on marked the opening of Port Patrick. "I did think I saw the jump o a porpoise."

He could see her conspiratorial smile as he looked down at her face over her shoulder, but she played along, straining to see into the water over by those cliffs.

"Good, good. That's the way. I hae always had motion sickness, ever since I was a child. My da taught me how tae fend it off, and ye dae hae the way o it. The trick is tae focus on something off in the distance, in the direction yer traveling."

It was pleasant standing behind her there. Her hair smelled like lilacs, but that wasna it. She just had an air about her that he found… comforting, like home. Well, and a bit exciting, too.

"Oh, but I dae see porpoises jumping oot there. We're closer now. Canna ye see them yet?"

"I can see them!"

Deirdre popped out of one of the crates piled up on deck. She laughed and climbed high up onto the bow, leaning forward so as to see them better.

"They're funny!"

Seumas went to grab her and pull her away from the certain peril of falling in front of the bow into the water and being run over by the ship.

Uncharacteristically, she ducked out of his grasp and was running back along the starboard side railing, stepping up on top of crates when she needed to in order to pass by, when the ship canted to starboard with the wind.

And quick as that, she went over the side and landed in the water with a splash and a scream.

"No!" Sasha yelled out as she ran over to the railing were Deirdre had gone over. Before Seumas realized what she was doing, she had climbed up on top of the same crate and dove off the side of the ship like one of the porpoises.

He yelled out to everyone around.

"The lassies went overboard!"

"The lassies went overboard!"

But no one paid him any mind. He grabbed the elbow closest to him and pulled the man attached around to face him.

"We need tae turn aroond and go back for them, ye hear?"

But the man's eyes were focused on something behind Seumas, and then Captain Dowd's voice boomed from there.

"We wull dae now such thing. If ye feel the need tae go back for them, then jump ower the side like yer fool lassie did."

If he was going to catch up with them before it was too late, then there wasn't time even to tell Tavish where he was going. Without a second thought, he was up on top of the crate and over the side himself, into the water with his own splash.

Swimming steadily toward where he could see Sasha bobbing in the water with Deirdre in tow, he felt foolish now for pointing out the porpoises jumping in the water. How had he missed Deirdre stowing herself away on board? Well, he had been rather busy loading cargo.

Sasha was making rather good progress toward the shore, and he had to veer to his left and triangulate so as not to miss her and be washed ashore too far down. She was aiming for the small beach where he and Alfred often swam as boys.

Now that he saw she wasn't in danger, he rather enjoyed watching her swim. She was strong and graceful. But then he saw that Deirdre wasn't moving, and he redoubled his efforts, hoping for he knew not what.

Sasha reached the beach before him, and she was fussing over poor Deirdre's lifeless body, turning it this way and that and patting on its back. Aw, now she was kissing the dead girl.

He swam as fast as he could, and the moment he reached the shore he ran for the stockpile of firewood he knew was there, piled up some tinder and dry leaves, and took his flint out of his sporran to spark the flame. As he worked, he called out to Sasha over his shoulder.

"I'm verra sorry for the loss o Deirdre, Sasha. Howsoever, ye need tae take care o yerself, ye ken? Mourn what yer gaun'ae mourn until I get this fire gang, but then come ower an warm yerself. Yer alive, and ye need tae take care o yerself tae ensure ye stay that way, aye?"

He was working on the fire and feeling sad that he couldn't look back to console her when she said some nonsensical thing about how the little girl was going to be fine and was breathing now and wait just wait a minute and she would bring her over. Best to nip her delusion in the bud.

"Weesht. I hae the fire gang now, but it will take a few minutes tae get warm enough tae dry yer clothes an warm ye up. We're gaun'ae have tae take oor clothes off and wring them oot sae they dry faster. I'm doing sae now while the fire gets hot. Fair warning. Cover yer eyes if ye like."

As soon as he was done with the fire and working on getting his kilt off to wring it out, he looked over to see how she was faring and froze, incredulous.

Just as she had said, Deirdre was up and walking over with her. They both had their heads bowed, and Sasha's arm was around the little girl, hugging her to her side. They were shivering with the cold.

He wrung the sea water out of his kilt and shirt as

quickly as he could and put them back on, then turned with his back to them and to the fire, enjoying its warmth while he figured out what to say to her.

She was clearly...

She...

She was using sorcery.

Did he care? He was nominally Catholic, as was everyone in Castleton. The church said that sorcery was evil, but he had seen... No, he had heard tales of how... Well, never mind. The bottom line was he didn't care if she was a sorceress or not, he was falling so deeply for her.

He swallowed and cleared his throat, still looking the other way.

"How are ye, Deirdre?"

The little girl's voice sounded harsh and choky, but she responded dutifully.

"Cold."

He nodded.

"Aye, the two o ye need tae remove yer clothing and wring oot all the moisture ye can and then put it back on and dry it ower the fire, like I am."

Sasha answered him, sparing the little girl the use of her sore voice.

"Aye, that we are doing. I know ye hae never seen a person resuscitated before. I can tell it upset ye. I'm guessing ye think it's ... I dinna ken if ye believe me when I tell ye this, but it is na. 'Tis... medicine, where I come from. Ye could dae it if I showed ye how." She was quiet for a few minutes while she and Deirdre finished putting their damp clothes back on. "Say something, sae I wull know how ye feel and what ye are thinking."

He took several deep breaths, still gazing at the

trees on the far side of the fire from her, unsure he ever wanted to turn around and see the evidence of her sorcery.

He didn't blame her for not admitting it.

"Deirdre, ye canna tell anyone what happened here, ye ken?"

The little girl started to speak, but Sasha shushed her.

"Weesht. Rest yer voice, dearie." And then she spoke to Seumas. "I Dinna ken why she shouldna tell the tale o me saving her from drowning. Anyone else would hae done the same, aye?"

"Aye," the little girl croaked out before Seumas could put two thoughts together.

Now he did turn around. If that was what the little girl thought, then it was brilliant. Ashamed at his relief in noticing the knife he had given Sasha was safely tucked in her belt and not at the bottom of the sea, he put a look of wonder on his face and crouched down so that he saw Deirdre eye to eye over the fire.

"Is that what happened? Did Sasha save ye from drowning?"

Deirdre nodded yes as she held her tiny arms out around the fire, almost like she was giving it a hug. She was still close to Sasha, and if they had dry clothes to change into, he was sure the two of them would be hugging each other for the fear of almost drowning.

He met Sasha's eyes, and they were pleading with him to just accept this about her and go back to the way they had been — was it not even an hour ago?

He couldn't think of any earthly thing to say, and he didn't trust his face to not reveal just how disturbed he was. So he did what he could to assure her that he wanted to go back to the way they had been. He walked around the fire to her side and took her hand in his and gently squeezed it. They stood there like that for an hour, making the kind of small talk Deirdre could repeat without causing alarm while they waited for their clothes to dry enough so that they wouldn't catch their deaths of cold on the walk back to Eileen's house in Castleton.

Naoi (9)

Once they were dry and the awkwardness of discussing CPR with a thirteenth century man had worn off, Sasha felt disappointed that they had to take Deirdre home and couldn't just continue on foot to meet Kelsey and Tavish at Turnberry Castle.

Anyway, Seumas said it was a two-day journey on foot and that she didn't have the boots for it, never mind that they would have to carry too much with them to go now, as the September nights were cold. Standing by the fire, that had sounded silly, but now walking back along the coast she felt the chill, even midday. She also felt every craggy rock through the thin souls of her dress boots.

Seumas carried Deirdre most of the way. The normally spry little girl was exhausted from her ordeal, and most of the time they could hear her snoring. This amused them and gave them a chance to talk. They spoke of everything except whether or not Sasha was a sorceress.

Seumas walked easily by her side, occasionally brushing the back of her hand with his.

"What dae ye fancy, at mealtime? Tell me the sort o feast ye most look forward tae?"

She'd always found it awkward discussing food with men, but he looked so earnest and so curious that this time she didn't mind.

"My mama has a way o fixing chicken I dearly love. She rubs eggs ower it and then rolls it in breadcrumbs, puts some butter in the pan, and fries it."

He hefted the sleeping girl in his arms to a more comfortable carrying position as he walked.

"Aye, that sounds good."

"What aboot ye?"

He freed one of his hands long enough to pat his stomach, then quickly caught Deirdre up close to his chest again.

"I fancy a good clam bake. What aboot games? Which games dae ye like tae play?"

She enjoyed gazing into his earnest eyes and seeing how genuinely he wanted to know.

"Dae ye mean ootside, or in the house after supper?"

He laughed.

"I did mean inside after supper, but ye have me curious. Dae ye yet play games ootside? And if sae, what are they?"

"Aye, I love tae play this game we hae where we make three places we need tae run tae before we come home again. We hold a stick, and the enemy throws at us a ball. We hit it as far as we can with the stick, and while they're running after the ball, we have tae run tae all three places and come home again."

He smiled warmly, nodding as he kicked a small stick up into the air and laughing when it landed in a tree and made several birds take flight.

"I hae playit such a game. When we were children, we playit an easy one where we put the ball on a stool and hit it off. Now, I prefer a good game o save the castle, such as Aodh, Niall, and even little Sile were playing when first ye saw them."

She found it surprisingly easy to talk with him.

During the times when Deirdre was awake, Sasha took her little wooden flute out of the pouch she kept it in and played some of her favorite songs for the two of them, pleasantly surprised to find that it still sounded good after the dunking it had received today. She was a little afraid Seumas and Deirdre would ask her to play some songs that were popular now, but thankfully they didn't. Whew.

If not for the severity of what had happened to Deirdre, Sasha would've considered this walk along the coastline and past the harbor a party. The sound of the ocean had always made her happy, and it was even better here. There were no other sounds to detract from it. No planes nor helicopters overhead. No automobiles with their noise and their stink. Just the birds chirping in the trees and the waves crashing on the beach.

And his voice.

Each time she met Seumas's eyes, she definitely wanted to celebrate the closeness she felt with him, as if they had known each other years instead of days. As if they were meant to be together.

So it was with slow steps and heavy hearts that they at last arrived at the weaver shop. Eileen took one look at them and gasped, reaching her arms out for her daughter.

"Deirdre, Deirdre, ye had me worried sick, and now ye come home looking like a drowned rat." She met Sasha's eyes, and when Sasha nodded, Eileen became distraught and headed for home, holding her daughter like a baby and rocking her. Aodh and Niall followed, and Sasha scooped up and carried Sile.

When they got home, Eileen carried Deirdre into the bedroom and laid her down to rest, cooing and fussing over her, and speaking to Sasha and Seumas over her shoulder.

"Ye wull excuse me if I dinna entertain ye, I'm sure."

"Aye," they both told her.

And then they spent a pleasant if tense afternoon playing games with Aodh, Niall, and Sile and making a passing if messy supper.

When Alfred arrived, he took one look at Eileen and Deirdre and nodded toward Seumas, who nodded back and got up to leave. While Alfred said his goodbyes to Eileen and gave her his sympathy for her daughter's illness, Seumas stood close to Sasha holding her hand and giving her hope and a promise with his eyes, but saying nothing at all except good night.

~*~

In her dream that night, Sasha found herself inside

Turnberry Castle with Kelsey. It was magnificent with high vaulted ceilings.

"I really think that Seumas and I should come join you. Four of us will be able to search much faster than two of you."

But Kelsey shook her head no with an odd smile on her face.

"No, Seumas is right. You need to stay put and wait for us to get back. It's too tough a journey and too risky with the cold. Besides, Eileen needs help now more than ever, with a sick daughter."

Her smile got bigger and she stood there waiting for Sasha to guess what she was smiling about. When Sasha shrugged, Kelsey held her hands out to the sides with her elbows bent.

"And anyway, I can explore much faster than all four of us put together ever could in real life—in my dreams. All I have to do is touch someone, and then I'm able to get into their dream with them…"

And that was that.

Sasha gave up any chance of meeting Kelsey at Turnberry Castle. She hung around with Kelsey in their shared dream for a while and got a tour at least, and then said she might as well go back to her body and get some good sleep.

Really, she was just jealous that Kelsey got to be in that other castle. She didn't really want to see too much of it in her dreams or she'd be too sorry she couldn't go.

~*~

Even though Kelsey had used Deirdre's illness as a reason for Sasha to stay put, Sasha was relieved when the little girl was better by morning.

She passed a normal day in the weaver shop, and

then another the next day, and another the next.

Frankly, she found day-to-day life in medieval times boring. At least for the working people it was. Her evenings were pleasant, playing games with Seumas and the children and talking and laughing with Alfred and Eileen. But the days. She felt like her head would explode with boredom if she had to spend one more whole day shredding flax plant into linen threads.

And wasn't there a castle right here that she might explore? Even better, wasn't there a man here who had some answers, when all Kelsey had were hints and guesses?

On the pretext of doing a little marketing, Sasha headed out at midday toward the castle. Brian the Druid knew things. She could tell. Maybe after being alone up there for a week, he would appreciate having company.

She was almost to the castle gate when someone in the street grabbed her arm and roughly yanked her toward himself, breathing rotten alcohol breath down her throat.

"Yer a big one, aren't ye. Come shew us a little— ack!"

Seumas grabbed the man and pushed him away down the street, where he tripped over his own feet from the momentum and fell down in a heap. Seumas stood there for a long moment staring the heap down, his chest heaving and his breath coming out ragged, his fists clenched and his arms bent.

"While Tavish is away, Sasha is under my protection, ye ken?"

The man stayed down in a heap and nodded.

Seumas relaxed a bit but didn't take his eyes off

her attacker. He moved around Sasha until he could see both her and the heap at the same time, looking her over with concern in his eyes.

"Are ye whole? Did he hurt ye?"

Realizing she was hugging herself, she let her arms fall to her sides naturally and took stock.

"Aye, I am whole. He didna get the chance tae hurt me, ye grabbed him sae fast."

He nodded, relaxing more but still not taking his eyes off the man — who still lay in a heap. No one was even helping the man, such was his reputation, she supposed. She resumed her walk into the castle, wondering if Seumas was going to try and stop her once he realized where she was going.

But he just looked sad as they passed through several long stone hallways and climbed six flights of spiraling tower stairs.

Brian the Druid's elderly face was looking through the bars of his thick wooden door — just like he had been in Kelsey's dream. And he remembered the dream, because he recognized her. She could tell by the look on his face.

Suddenly glad she'd brought Seumas along, she took the huge kilted warrior's hand as they walked up the last flight of steps.

He held her hand. Tensely, but he held it.

Brian threw his head back inside his tower prison and burst out laughing. He laughed from his gut for almost a minute in fits and starts, making his long white beard bounce against his white cleric's robe. He would start to speak, and then he would be laughing again. Finally, he resumed his spot with his face pressing against the bars of the door, but his mouth was scrunched up in amusement.

When he spoke, he kept shaking with pent-up laughter. If she didn't know he'd been locked up for trying to molest her friend, she might have found him fun, rather than creepy.

"Heard aboot yer little mishap on the ship. Sae sad aboot the wee lass. Och, but she didna drown, did she? Now I wonder how that could be. Someone has an uncanny skill, never heard o before. Almost as if she had seen the future."

Sasha's heart raced, and she felt adrenaline zooming through her body.

What was the old Druid doing? Seumas couldn't be allowed to know the druids could make people travel through time.

Sasha turned around to go back down the stairs.

"I don't know why I came up here. That man is clearly daft. No way to get answers from someone who's lost his mind."

Not letting go of her hand, Seumas quietly persisted in staying with her as she started down the stairs. Any moment now, he would ask her what she was doing up here anyway.

What should she tell him? Best to keep to Kelsey's cover story about Sasha's grandmother telling Sasha to investigate the legend of the sword.

But Brian called out after her, making her an offer she couldn't refuse.

"I ken where the sword is, the one Kelsey and Tavish need."

She stopped dead in her tracks and then turned the top half of her body around to look at the white-haired druid from halfway down the staircase.

"Ye dae?"

Brian laughed some more.

"Aye, I dae. And all it will cost ye is the exchange o yer knowledge for mine."

Her heart was still racing. She was very aware that the man was dangerous. And something about the way he had phrased that raised up the hair on her arms.

It must have alarmed Seumas too, because he let go of her hand and turned so that he could hold her by the waist—hold her back from climbing the stairs again.

She was glad. She had been about to rush back up the stairs toward Brian, and if he wanted to, he could reach through the bars. They could hear each other just fine from this distance, and they were up far enough in the tower that no one else could hear them unless they came up the stairs. She would hear anyone who came up the stairs behind her. The tower echoed.

Relaxing into Seumas's strong embrace and letting it calm and reassure her, she considered her words carefully. Many of the Celtic fairy tales she had read for her studies included battles of wits, and often some poor soul agreed to something unimagined.

At last she arrived on what she thought was the best question to ask.

"How much of my knowledge would you require in order to tell me where the sword that Tavish needs is?"

The Druid laughed again, but when he saw that it wasn't getting to her this time, he abruptly stopped.

"Clever lass. Ye need only tae answer my questions first."

Something about the way he said it calmed her and made her relax. Answering his questions wouldn't be dangerous.

But Seumas gently squeezed her to him, distracting her attention away from Brian.

Watch it, her caution screamed at her. Be careful. Druids have magic, and this one also has something up his sleeve.

She swallowed and again carefully considered her answer.

"How many of your questions would I need to answer?"

Brian backed away from the barred window a bit, smiling a knowing smile.

"Ah, now we are getting doon tae it. Ye have decidit tae answer my questions. Now 'tis only a matter o dithering ower quantities."

She gasped, and a new shot of adrenaline rushed through her.

"I didna agree tae anything."

"Nay, not yet, but ye wull."

Seumas gave her waist a tentative tug toward the bottom of the stairs. Bless the man for respecting her enough to let her decide if they were leaving or not. She could tell he was itching to be on their way. But what danger were they in? Brian couldn't reach them this far down the stairs.

She patted Seumas's hand on her waist but stayed put, having a stare-out with Brian.

"Wull, how many questions o yers will I need tae answer before ye tell me where the sword is that Tavish needs?"

Brian smiled huge, showing all his rotting teeth, and rubbing his hands together in odd patterns.

"Och, I say we go with the customary three, eh? Answer me three questions, and I shall tell ye where the sword is that Tavish needs."

Sasha stood there for a long moment, considering her response. She hadn't agreed to give him all of her knowledge. That could've been disastrous for her. She had a picture of him sucking all the knowledge out of her head, leaving her an idiot.

Yes, she was sure she wasn't leaving herself open to that when she replied, sneaking in a little extra knowledge for herself.

"Agreed. I wull answer three o yer questions, and then ye wull tell me where the sword is that Tavish needs — and ye wull answer two o my questions about the Druids."

Victory shown in Brian's eyes and his smile got huge and a little bit evil.

"Agreed. Question the first. How is it ye came tae own that ring, the one that marks ye as a druid priestess?"

Sasha's adrenaline was all used up by now, so all she could do was gasp at the trouble the old Druid was bringing down on her head. She tried to speak, but found she couldn't. Her mouth was sealed shut and her tongue wouldn't move. She forgotten about this part of the fairytales. Only a few had this malady. Why had she forgotten? She tried to turn and go down the stairs, but felt she couldn't move either. Her feet were frozen to their place on the stairway.

To his credit, Seumas yet stayed with her, even though she had the impression that he could leave if he wanted to. But his embrace felt mechanical now, rather than warm and affectionate as it had before.

Giddily, the old Druid went on condemning her in Seumas's hearing.

"Question the second. How far intae the future

are ye from, Sasha? And if ye dinna mind me asking, tell an old man aboot all the wonders yer life has seen in yer own time."

Tears welled up in Sasha's eyes, and a lump formed in her throat that she had no ability to swallow. Her throat burned, and she started sobbing. Just like that, the old man had ruined any chance she had with Seumas. Again she tried to leave, but again she was prevented by Brian's magic.

And again, Seumas stood by her. Hope bloomed in her heart afresh. Maybe he loved her. Maybe they could be together anyway. She braced herself for the one last question. As soon as he spoke it, she would answer all three questions in rapid succession and then ask him about the sword and get the hell out of there. Heck with finding out more about the Druids.

Brian was shaking with glee now, and through the bars in the wooden door, his eyes absolutely radiated victory.

"Question the third. Which type o our druidic magic is yer specialty, Sorceress?"

Deich (10)

Her sobs were coming repeatedly now, racking her whole body so that she would've collapsed if Seumas hadn't been holding her. Forget never having a chance with him. Now a small kernel of fear blossomed in her heart. He would be sure she not only was a sorceress, but also was hiding it from him and had lied to him. What would he do to her?

Brian positively cackled with laughter now.

"What's the matter? Did the cat come and steal yer tongue away? An agreement is an agreement. All ye have tae dae is answer my questions, and I wull answer yers." He cackled some more.

She was in an impossible situation. She could move now. Her limbs had been freed. And she could speak now if she wanted. But what would she say? And where would she go?

After his cruelty in driving such a wedge between her and Seumas, she couldn't bear to speak to Brian again. No way would she answer his questions. They would just have to find the sword through other means. Perhaps Tavish and Kelsey would find it all on their own.

And she would certainly find another way to inquire about what it meant to be a druid. A surge of anger ran through her, directed at their professors at Celtic University. If they were going to make her and Kelsey into Druids, the least they could've done was tell them what it meant. How dare they send them off on these quests without even knowing what they were or who they could trust or what they were meant to do with their knowledge?

That small kernel of anger propelled her feet, and she started to walk down the stairs.

Seumas came with her, incredibly still holding her gently by the waist. He didn't say a word, though, and she was starting to think that was a good thing. She often let her mouth run before her brain caught up with it. Good on him for thinking before he spoke.

They went down the spiraling stone staircase of the tower. A few moments before they got to the door at the bottom, the one that led out into the hall the Castle, she figured she had better speak to him while they still had privacy. She stopped, but didn't turn her head to him. Instead she looked at the stone floor, marveling at how it was made of thousands of tiny stones fit together with barely anything between them. In the back of her mind, she wondered at the ingredients of the sealant that was used to make such a floor in medieval times. Meanwhile, her mouth was running on.

"'Tis true I'm from the future. Tavish and Kelsey are tae. We are from eight hundred years in the future, in case ye were wondering. There isna way I'm gaun'ae tell Brian any o this, but I want ye tae know. I'm nay sorceress, na matter what it looks like or what he says. Though this ring I wear…"

She twisted the ring she wore on her right hand, the one she had been so proud of a few months ago when she was awarded it from Celtic University. Wrought from the purest silver, it looked like three pieces of thread woven together in Celtic knots of such intricacy that the eye couldn't follow all the lines of them.

"This is my ring I got for studying seven years at a Celtic place o learning. I thought it verra prestigious at the time. Now I come tae find oot the place is run by druids and that this marks me as a druid priestess. I know ye willna believe me, but I have na idea what it means tae be a druid priestess. They didna tell me I was studying tae be a druid priestess. All they said was I would be a doctor o Celtic archaeology. That means in my time, I find the ruins o places like this and dig them up and find items inside which tell the story o the people who lived long ago. Kelsey and I are digging oot the verra underground tunnels ye go intae all the time. Wull, in our time na one's been there for hundrits o years. 'Tis verra exciting and we're getting attention from all ower the waurld for it. I guess I'd better explain. In my time, we have stuff callit technology. It's verra complicated. I dinna understand how it works. It might as wull be magic, really, as much as I understand it. Anyhow, technology allows everyone in the waurld tae speak with each other, even tae see each other across vast distances. And a great many people can see one person ... 'Tis pointless for me tae go intae what 'tis all called. 'Tis just... 'Tis an honor tae be one o the people who speaks tae masses o people all around the waurld. And 'tis... fun. I really enjoy being the center o attention while I open one o the secret doors in the underground castle in front o all the waurld. I enjoy the admiration and awe and respect. But now 'tis all ruinit. Now ye think I'm a sorceress, and I almost wouldn't blame ye if ye felt like stoning me tae death or something."

She stood there and waited for him to say something, but he didn't. All he did was stand still with his arm still around her and nudge her a little bit on the waist, toward the door.

So she sighed deeply and headed out into the castle proper, unsure whether she was being consoled — or marched to the slaughter.

On the way through the door into the hallway, he dropped his hand from her waist. They walked the whole way back to the weaver shop in silence. She kept wanting to ask him to say something, but then fear took over and she didn't. Maybe if she pestered him about it he would explode. That was the pattern between her parents.

But the silence was maddening.

What was he thinking?

Did he hate her?

She kept her eyes on the ground in front of her the whole time, and when they arrived at the weaver shop door, she looked up to thank him for walking her back. But he was already walking away with his back to her.

Tears welled up in her eyes anew, and that choking feeling came back. She was deciding whether to go in or run back to Eileen's house to cry in private when the door opened.

All the children ran out into the street, laughing and playing a game of chase where they yelled a phrase at each other over and over.

"Galdus is gaun'ae get ye!"

The first time she heard it, she didn't understand what they were saying, they were so young and their accents were so thick and they were sing-songing it. But she heard it over and over again.

"Galdus is gaun'ae get ye!"

Hadn't Brian said something about Galdus when he saw the sword Kelsey was holding in her dream, the one that Tavish needed? Sasha went inside and picked up some of the flax that Eileen was shredding into thread so that Fergus could make linen.

"What does it mean, what the children are yelling at each oother aboot Galdus getting them?"

Eileen kept her hands on the flax and shrugged her shoulder.

"I dinna ken. It's an auld children's game we all played when we were young."

Fergus spoke up from his place at the loom.

"Galdus was an auld King. He's buried at Torhousekie, ye ken." He gestured to the east with his head, never taking his hands off his work.

Sasha's heart raced now in a good way. Brian had said Galdus's name when he saw Kelsey with the sword. Had he thought she was the old king come to life? Maybe they would find the sword at Galdus's burial site. Maybe the Robert the Bruce story was a red herring and Tavish and Kelsey were after the wrong sword.

She went over to Fergus's loom.

"Dae ye hae a preferred way tae get tae Torhousekie?"

Fergus looked up, visibly surprised.

"Ye know it?"

You have no idea. All the vast catalogues of sites she had studied for her doctorate whooshed before her eyes. The Torhouse Standing Stones were one of the first sites she'd been taught. But she mentally chastised herself for slipping up again and letting too much knowledge show.

Putting on the air of innocence, she raised her palms up to her sides with her elbows bent.

"My grandmother knows all sorts o stories."

Fergus went back to his work.

"The trail starts at Port Patrick. Most o us hae been at least once. It's a favorite trip for children on All Souls' Day."

"Och, Aye" she said to him. "I can well imagine."

Fergus seemed shy about her standing there, so she nodded to Uilleam and went back to her seat, but she had a hard time settling down to work.

Eileen reached across their table and took Sasha's hand.

"Ye hae been crying, and I did see Seumas walking away. Dae ye want tae talk aboot it?"

No, she didn't want to talk about it. And what was she going to do about it? For all she knew, Seumas would come back in a few minutes with a bunch of guards and arrest her and throw her in a dungeon —

or worse.

"Nah, but would ye mind a great deal if I went back tae the house and..."

Eileen put her work down and got up and helped Sasha up and gave her a warm hug.

"Go on, then. I can dae fine here." She smiled weakly at Sasha and squeezed her hands, then let go and went back to her work.

So that was it. Sasha was free to go. And she couldn't say goodbye to Eileen, nor to Deirdre — who could still be heard outside yelling and playing with her brothers and sister.

Sasha gathered her purse and cloak, resisted the urge to look longingly at her suit there in the bucket, then made her way outside and hurried down the street before the children noticed her and asked questions. She walked toward Eileen's house at first, just in case Eileen looked out the door to watch her go. As soon as she rounded the first corner though, she headed toward Port Patrick. There were food vendors there, and she had a week's wages to spend.

She would get as far as she could today, and then she'd consult with Kelsey in her dreams tonight on how to meet up with her and Tavish — and she would tell her what happened. They had to come back here to go home — and she really wanted to get her suit back — but they'd worry about that later. For now, she would go to Torhousekie and see if she could find Galdus's sword.

And avoid death by highlander.

~*~

Oh yeah. Her boots were not good walking boots at all. She felt every rock on every step. The only things she was carrying were a thick wool blanket and a small gunnysack of cheese and apples that she'd bought. And she was exhausted after walking only six of the nine hours to Torhousekie. She hoped she had put enough distance between her and Dunskey Castle so that she could rest for the night.

For the past half-hour she'd been looking for any sort of shelter where she might spend the night and not be attacked by wild animals. What kind of wild animals did they have in Scotland in the twelve hundreds, anyway? She didn't have a clue, but she didn't want to leave her throat bare.

At long last, she found a bush the size of a car and crawled in between its branches and lay down with her back against the trunk. It was so uncomfortable that she lay there a long time before she finally fell asleep. To alleviate the boredom, she ate another portion of her cheese and apples while waiting for sleep to take her.

~*~

In her dream, Sasha entered Turnberry Castle. She could tell it wasn't a normal dream. In normal dreams, she wasn't given a tour. It was a grand place full of warm fireplaces and views of the sea cliffs, and she couldn't wait to get there.

Kelsey took one look at Sasha's face and became all concerned.

"What's wrong?"

Sasha leaned out one of the arrow slit windows to feel the impossible warm sunlight and smell the fresh sea breeze.

"Seumas came with me to see Brian, and the Druid told him all about time travel."

Kelsey was suddenly right behind. Her voice sounded concerned, but not panicky. She didn't get it.

"Isn't that good? At least you don't have a secret from him anymore."

Sasha turned around so that Kelsey would see how worried she was, how afraid, how much she needed to come join her and Tavish.

"No, he thinks I'm a sorceress — and I guess I am, right?"

Kelsey vehemently shook her head.

"No."

Sasha put her hands on her hips. Feeling foolish as soon as she did so in light of Deirdre's habit, she instead gestured back and forth between the two of them, then around in include the castle.

"Well what do you call this thing we're doing right now?"

Kelsey opened her mouth to speak, closed it, grunted, and then spoke after all.

"I don't know, but we're not practicing sorcery."

Sasha turned to pace into the next room of this luxurious upstairs castle suite.

"Well he thinks I'm a sorceress, and you should've seen him, Kelsey, talking about sorcery earlier. I just barely convinced him I wasn't a witch. And now he thinks I am, and ... I left there, Kelsey. I'm six hours east on my way to Torhousekie standing stones — because the children were playing a game about how Galdus is going to get you and Fergus says Galdus is buried at Torhousekie and then I remembered what Brian said when he saw you with the sword. He said, 'Galdus?' Remember?"

Kelsey raised her eyebrows.

"Yeah, he did say Galdus."

Sasha nodded.

"So tomorrow I'll go check it out, and after that

I'm coming to stay with you guys there …"

~*~

Sasha woke up in the middle of the night, shivering with cold right through her wool blanket and needing to relieve herself. The latter was easy to take care of, the former not so much. She dug through every last compartment of her purse, hoping it was still in there. All sorts of things she would normally be happy to find gave her no joy at all: chewing gum, a favorite lipstick, breath mints… Aha. Triumphantly, she wrapped her hand around a matchbook from Jack in the Green, a cool club near campus. She left it in her purse for now.

Okay, how hard could it be to build a fire?

She looked around her surprisingly easy-to-see surroundings for firewood. When she first woke up, it had seemed pitch black, but now she could see fine under just a few stars and the moon. Who knew?

She gathered all the firewood she could find and put it in a clear area a bit away from the bush where she'd slept. Carefully, she took the matchbook out of her purse, knelt down beside the firewood, lit a match …

And the wind blew it out.

Inspiration struck. She took the blanket and put it over her head and then lowered herself over the wood… And it was pitch black.

Oh well. She lowered the matchbook down close to the wood under the blanket out of the wind and lit a match by touch. Yay! She could see, and the match didn't blow out. She held it next to the wood… And had to let go before it burned her fingers.

Okay, she needed to light something else with the match, something that would light easily and stay lit long enough to light the wood on fire. She hated to go outside of her little blanket tent into the wind, but it felt like if she didn't get a fire lit she would freeze to death.

Ooh, there were a bunch of dry leaves all over the ground. They were only slightly damp. No damper than the wood, really. She looked gratefully over at the bush's large leaves, glad her bed had been dry.

She gathered a bunch of leaves and put them in the middle of the circle she'd made with her wood — and finally saw some flames. Not much, though. Not enough that she felt like she had to raise up her blanket tent away from the fire.

Then she coughed.

Ugh, it was getting smoky in here.

She tried something she'd seen in a movie once and blew on the smoky leaves that were close to one of the pieces of wood. That made a satisfying flare of light, so she tried that again. At least this time the fire was staying lit and wasn't going out.

But it was getting way too smoky. She was going to have to take the blanket away and let the wind in. She felt the wind mostly coming from her left, so she moved in that direction to try and block it from getting the fire. In desperation, she held out her arms under the blanket and made sort of a wall that could block the wind from getting to her tiny smoky little fire.

Blowing on it had helped. She knelt down and kept gently blowing on the smoldering leaves near the damp wood as much as she could between breaths of smoky air.

Uh oh.

Almost all the leaves were burned up, and the

wood still wasn't really burning, just smoking. She made a mad dash for more leaves, having to go pretty far away this time because she had gathered all the leaves that were close by already. She ran back with an armful of leaves, wondering how she was going to put them on the burning leaves without smothering them.

And her fire had gone out.

She fished out the matchbook and counted how many matches she had left. Thirteen. And she would have to spend at least one more night out in the open before she got to Kelsey. She needed to be smarter about this.

Using the blanket as a bag, she went far and wide, foraging all around the area for as many leaves as she could carry, then stacked most of them a few steps away from where she was making her fire.

She hadn't been too careful about gathering the leaves, and a whole bunch of small sticks were in the pile. She discovered kindling wood by accident because of this, and after that it was pretty easy to keep the fire going. The big wood even caught in one place, but it was still more smoke than fire. Maybe if she—

She sat up straight.

What was that noise?

She looked all around but didn't see anything moving.

Darn, she couldn't see outside the little ring of light from her fire. Wasn't fire supposed to keep animals away? She definitely heard a twig snap. Her heart raced, and she looked over toward the bush. It would provide some protection, unlike sitting out here with her back exposed.

She hated to leave the fire, but all of her instincts were telling her to go back into the bush. She grabbed her purse and crawled in there, suddenly gasping for breath in a panic at what was coming.

Aon Deug (11)

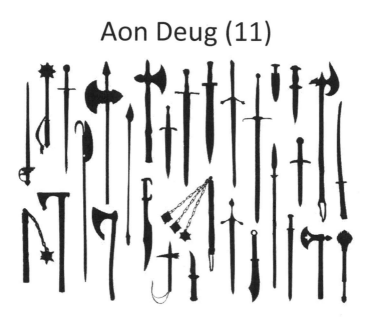

The scent of smoke was getting stronger now, so he was going the right way. He hurried a little. The scent was of damp leaves burning, rather than wood. The fire couldn't be very warm, and the weather was cold this time of night. He could see his breath. Aye, he was getting quite close now. She was probably camped inside the great bush where he and Alfred had slept the summer they made their trek out here as children. It was a common campsite. Everyone knew it.

He went over the rise, and there it was, her fire — if it could be called that. But she wasn't by the fire.

She was inside the bush, trembling.

His throat had become hoarse long ago from yelling out her name, and now he took a long drink from the water skin he carried before trying it again.

"Sasha, it's me, Seumas! Come oot!"

He couldn't believe his eyes. Instead of coming out, she was crawling around to the other side of the bush. By now, he was close enough that he no longer had to yell, thank the Saints.

"Where are ye going? Ye dinna hae tae hide. 'Tis only me. Come on oot, Sasha."

It slowly dawned that it was him she feared.

His hands sank to his sides, and his lungs deflated. His anger was why she wasn't out by her fire, why she sat trembling in the bush, probably with cold as well as fear.

He approached slowly, not making any sudden moves, until he could make quick work of salvaging her fire and building it up so that it was actually warm. Once that was done and it no longer threatened to go out, he built another fire a few feet away so they might sit between the two and be warm on both sides. He sat down on the far side of the fires facing her, so that she could see him well. Then he took off all his weapons and cast them aside.

He cleared his throat, drank some more water, and tried his best to let his apology be heard in the tone of his voice.

"I ken that I went away angry. I'm sae sorry. Howsoever, never in a thousand years would I hae guessed ye'd leave the safety of oor castle town on yer own. When Eileen got home and ye weren't there, she didna worry. She figured ye and I had made peace and ye had gone oot with me. But when Alfred arrived and said he'd been with me… It was then she telt me ye had asked aboot Galdus shortly after ye and I parted. And I kenned ye had come oot here all on yer own tae seek oot Galdus's burial place for yerself. I came tae make sure ye were warm enough, and now yer hiding from my fire. Please come oot and warm yerself. I wull back away if ye like, but ye mustna get ower cauld. Ye wull catch yer death."

He got up and backed away, true to his word, and sat down again at a safe distance.

"There. Now ye can come oot with na worry."

She did crawl out then and make her way between the fires to sit down and warm herself, thank all that was holy. But she still didn't speak. She didn't even look at him, just sat between the two fires, shivering less and less.

Any moment now, she would ask him to leave. He rushed into the rest of his apology, earnest to get it out while he could — and only barely daring to hope she would accept it and agree to travel together.

"Sae glad ye are warming yerself. I've had many hours tae think, walking here alone. And the more I thought, the more I realized the ring o truth was in yer voice when ye assured me ye were no a sorceress. Sae even though the workings o sorcery surround ye, I dae believe ye. I mean ye na harm, I —"

At last she spoke, cutting him off.

"I believe ye as well. Now go and get yer weapons and come ower here where it's warm! Ye had me at," she imitated his voice, "'now yer hiding from my fire.'" And then she burst out laughing.

At the sound of her laughter, an overwhelming wave of relief washed over him, and he slid over to her on his bottom, so as to keep his face level with hers and eliminate any doubts that might be lingering in her mind, about whether he meant her harm. The rocks and twigs stuck to his kilt and cut into his buttocks, but he didn't care.

At last, he was by her side.

Her smile and her dancing eyes were radiant in the firelight, inviting his kiss.

His heart leapt!

Just to be sure, he moved in slowly, keeping his eyes on hers, which smiled more and more the closer he got.

And so their lips met — gently, tenderly. But they soon turned it into a wanting kiss, a promising kiss. A kiss whose fire rivaled the blazes on either side of them.

At first, he thought Sasha was giggling as she kissed him. He'd never had that effect on a woman before, but there was nothing about Sasha that didn't surprise him, so he went with it.

But then his body was close enough to hers that he should've felt it if she were giggling. And he knew it wasn't her.

With a sigh, he drew away and sat up.

"Did ye follow me here, Deirdre?"

The little girl stood across from one of the fires, leaning over and warming herself. She had a big smile on her face and a big cloak wrapped around her little body, so she seemed to be fine, but guilt racked him at not noticing she was following him before he got this far away from her mother.

Still giggling, she nodded her tiny head, bobbing her cute little blonde curls.

Seumas sighed and turned to Sasha.

"Wull, get yerself warmit up and then we can take

her home. I hope ye restit enough. I havena, but I am more accustomit tae walking."

Oh no.

He knew that look. Determination was blooming inside her. This could not be good.

She lowered her forehead and raised her eyebrows.

"Yer the one she followit here, sae if anyone's takin her home, ye are. Howsoever, I'm gaun'ae Torhousekie and see aboot auld King Galdus's sword."

He raised his chin for extra authority and opened his mouth to tell her no, that it was too dangerous for her to be out alone.

But she did an odd thing and dashed her eyes over to Deirdre and back before she continued speaking. She also wrinkled her forehead at him and gave him an intense stare.

"I'm beginning tae think my grandmother was on tae something, when she telt me tae find the sword. It might be verra important, na only for me, but also for Tavish and Kelsey. I fact, I ken that tae be sae. It wouldna be..." She did that eye-dart thing over to Deirdre again, telling him she was guarding her words for the sake of not telling the wee one of her and Tavish and Kelsey's servitude to the druids. "It wouldna be healthy for us tae na find the sword. Sae I'm going, whether ye come with me or no."

He couldn't let her go alone. She would die for sure. Traits that he had thought derived from her nobility — flawless skin, filled out cheeks, bright white eyes and teeth — now made more sense to him as the traits of a person who lived in a much easier time. A time when those machines she had spoken of did all the hard physical work.

She hadn't discussed it, but he knew without a shadow of a doubt that she had never killed anything, not even for food. She had never worked at hard labor, and she certainly had never walked any great distance.

He held out his water skin to her.

"Here, ye must be thirsty."

She rolled her eyes and took it from him grudgingly, but once she had started, she drank almost all the water before she handed it back and he gave it to Deirdre, who took a sip and handed it back immediately, wrinkling her nose at how silly Sasha was. He winked at the little girl.

"Thank ye," Sasha said. And then her mouth formed a line on her face, and she looked thoughtful. "I brought food," she gestured over at the bush, "but I didna hae anything tae carry water in." She took hold of a stick that lay nearby and stirred the fire around as if it were stew.

Deirdre ran over to the bush and came back with a bag that she held open to show a few apples and a lump of cheese. She started to get out one of the apples, but he shook his head no at her. She put it back and sat down close beside Sasha, who put an arm around her and hugged her close.

He turned his water skin over and over in his hands.

"This is a cow's bladder. Howsoever, ye can use any bladder as a water skin. The kind o animal ye can get depends upon the weapon ye have. What weapons hae ye?"

The line of her mouth deepened and her eyebrows furled again as she looked down at her waist.

"All I hae is the knife ye gave me." Inspiration

must've struck her, because she raised her eyebrows and opened her mouth in a smile when she looked up at him. "But I could use it as a spearhead, couldna I?"

Heh, she wasn't entirely ignorant, but her knowledge was the kind heard around campfires and in busy pubs — or read in the pages of a rare cherished book — not the practical kind of knowledge you needed to travel on your own.

His mind whorled with the implications, trying to imagine a time when even a grown lass such as Sasha didn't know these things. He and Alfred had only been ten and twelve when the two of them traveled here on their own.

However.

He looked at Sasha's proud face.

He knew her type, albeit among men. She wouldn't listen if he tried to tell her she lacked skills. She was proud. It was one of the things he liked about her — that, and how impulsive she was. But her pride would get in the way if he tried to teach her directly. It was best to humor her.

So he nodded and gave her the closemouthed smile of someone who was impressed.

"Aye, that ye could. What wull ye use tae tie the knife ontae the long stick as a spearhead?"

She licked her lips and looked all around, as if she would find a leather strap in one of the trees. She was adorable, and it was difficult to keep a serious face.

Her eyes finally landed on her boots, and then she looked up at him triumphantly, smiling.

"I could use one o my shoelaces."

Ridiculous. Those laces looked to be made of some fiber that would never shrink to tighten with water the way leather would. If she were anyone else

. . .

But that was the point, wasn't it? She wasn't anyone else. She was Sasha the time traveler, wise in her own time and helpless in his.

But pride is a weakness that wounds deeply when pierced. No, he wouldn't do that to her. Not if he could help it. He shrugged a little, and looked around at all the materials available.

"Mayhap ye had best dae sae before we settle doon for the night, ye ken?"

On hearing him call her bluff, she bit her lip and got up, looking around rather forlornly — and adorably. She first went over to the bush and examined its long branches. She did this for quite a while, and he chuckled and sighed. This was going to be easy. Those branches were way too flexible. There would be no way to stab at your dinner.

Oh, but she tested one of them and saw this for herself. He found himself smiling, proud of her. She was a clever lass. He had never doubted that.

Deirdre scooted over toward him and curled up against his side, then whispered up at him.

"If we canna eat the apples and cheese, what can we eat? I'm sae hungry my tum is growling."

He opened the pouch that dangled at his belt, and she squealed in delight and reached in and took out some jerky and dried fruit, then munched happily.

Finally, Sasha came back to the fires and picked up the stick she'd been stirring with earlier. It wasn't so long as the bush limbs, only about the length of her leg, but it was straight and sturdy.

He nodded at her.

"Ye hae made a good choice for the shaft o yer spear. Now let us see ye fasten the knife tae it."

She fumbled just getting her knife out of her belt, and he had to stifle a laugh by blowing his nose in his sleeve.

Deirdre had caught on to the game, and she covered her mouth to stifle her own giggles, then reached for his water skin. Once she had emptied it down her throat, she handed it back and curled up next to him between the two fires with her head resting on his leg. He undid his arisade and opened it up so that it covered both of them, and the little girl sighed and closed her eyes.

Meanwhile, Sasha had gotten the knife off her belt and was fumbling around with things in her little bag with her back turned to him. Interesting.

After a while, she turned back around again, triumphant.

"I did it. See?" She held up the spear she had made.

He reached out his hand, and she gave it to him to examine.

Much to his surprise, he had to admire her spear. The knife stayed firmly in place. It wasn't a strong enough connection to hold against deer hide, but it wasn't meant to. She could kill something small with it and have a meal.

"I hae tae admit, this is a far better spear than I imaginit ye would make. What is this material that holds the knife tae the stick sae well without having tae be shrunk on it like leather?"

Her face was glowing with his praise, making her look especially beautiful — and that was saying something, because the firelight glinting on her long red hair and the moon shimmering in her eyes were already weaving their magic on him.

She smiled, and it looked mischievous.

"I ken, it's cheating. But all's fair in love and war, aye? They are callit rubber bands. They are meant tae keep my hair up, and sae they are coverit with a layer o silky thread. Otherwise, my hair would stick tae them and tear. They work verra well for making a spear, dinna they?"

When she looked away to swat a bug, he pulled on one of the rubber bands a bit. It sprang back to the knife with a loud snapping sound. He looked up to see if she had heard, but she was studying the spot on her wrist where the bug had been. He absentmindedly turned the spear this way and that to examine the rubber bands in the firelight.

"I dinna fancy admitting this tae ye, but I hae a strong urge tae cut these rubber bands open and see what's inside." He gave her his own sheepish smile and handed her spear back.

She laid the spear down by the rocks he had put round the fire and fished in her little bag some more. At last, she brought a tiny little thing out and handed it to him.

It was the color of snot, and about the same consistency. He could hear his mother scolding him for playing with it. That was how much it resembled the stuff. Nonetheless, he played with it for quite a while, laughing.

But when Deirdre opened her eyes for a moment, he quit and gave the rubber band back to Sasha, then stroked Deirdre's hair to encourage her to settle down again.

"Rubber. Does it come from an animal?"

Sasha gave him an understanding smile.

Which made him realize how arrogant he had been

just a few moments ago, laughing at her ignorance of things he took for granted. There were just as many things she knew that he didn't — far more things, mayhap. Machines and technology. Communicating with all the world…

She was speaking.

"Nay, it comes from a tree that grows doon in the jungles near the equator."

"The equator?"

She drew with her finger in the dirt.

"An imaginit ring round the fat part o the waurld, the warmest part — far away from here."

He laughed.

"Aye, the ships' crewmen tell stories o lands warmer than here, saying there are far more warmer than caulder, here in Scotland. Hae ye been tae many o them?"

She looked up at the stars, collecting her thoughts, and he took the opportunity to admire the pleasing lines of her face, brought out by the firelight. After a moment she looked back at him and sparkled her eyes, nodding yes.

"I hae been tae a dozen o them or more. I lived in one o those places with my parents in my early teens."

He took her hand and guided her over on the other side of him from Deirdre, then lay down and waited for her to lie down as well.

She squeezed his hand, got up, and came back with one of Cottman Brogan's fine woolen blankets, which she wrapped around herself before lying down next to him.

"Are we gaun'ae sleep while these fires yet burn? Isna that dangerous?"

"A bit," he said. "But it would be more dangerous trying tae sleep without the fires. 'Tis quite cauld. Rest ye easy. They're doon tae coals, but the sun will be up before they go oot."

Dà Dheug (12)

Sasha woke up cramped and uncomfortable, reaching to pull herself back up onto her bed. Must've had too much to drink last night. This always happened when she did. She couldn't reach the bed. She opened her eyes to find it — and came fully awake, gasping. Where the ...

Oh yeah.

Seumas!

Content and feeling safe now that she saw his back, she relaxed and took in the wonderful sights and scents of nature around her, covered by smoke and fire — and the aroma of roasting meat.

She swallowed. Her mouth was watering despite all

the smoke from fat dripping into the fire.

When she sat up, she had to rub her eyes to believe what she saw. Seumas and Deirdre were indeed roasting meat over a fire – on her spear.

She grabbed her purse. Best to make herself presentable before he saw that she was awake. She washed her face with a moist towelette and brushed out her hair. After she had applied the quickest version of makeup she could manage, she felt presentable. Barely.

"Couldna wait tae test my spear oot, eh Seumas? How was it?"

He gave her a goofy look that made her giggle and then walked over to offer his hand.

She let him help her up, and they embraced. It felt so good, it was making her delirious. She melted into him.

And then they heard Deirdre's giggling again.

Oh yeah. They weren't alone. Her body wasn't as willing to let go as her mind was, and their separation was slow and gradual and reluctant. Finally, though, they were only holding hands, watching Deirdre roast the meat like an expert.

The way she handled the spear really was quite amazing. It was the perfect size for her, so that it looked like it had been made for her.

And then it dawned on Sasha.

"No way."

She was so amazed, she had slipped into English by accident. Deirdre looked at her quizzically, but Seumas clearly understood what she'd said.

"Aye, the wee lass caught the rabbit, not I. She's a fine little huntress."

They had a hearty breakfast of roasted meat

complemented with her apples and cheese, washed down with fresh water Seumas had walked a mile and back to fetch for them all.

The whole time, Sasha was doing her best not to feel inadequate. It was difficult, being bested by a six-year-old. No, Sasha hadn't tried and failed. That wasn't the point. Deirdre had been up at dawn and gone out and gotten them food, and Sasha had slept in.

But once the food was in her stomach and they strapped what little they had to themselves and were on their way, she gradually got over it. Walking with Deirdre and Seumas was far better than walking by herself.

Deirdre was entertaining, for one thing. She literally ran circles around Sasha and Seumas, checking out every thistle bush and oddly shaped rock until she suddenly was just too tired to walk anymore and Seumas scooped her up and carried her in his arms the rest of the way, snoring again.

They exchanged a look over the sleeping girl as they walked.

"Aye," Sasha said to him, "this is nice. It feels like we're a family."

Seumas kissed the top of Deirdre's head as he crested a hill.

"Ye took the words oot o my mouth."

Sasha looked tenderly at Deirdre.

"Poor dear. She was up most o the night chasing after ye, and then she was sae excited tae be underway with us this morning that she wore herself oot."

They went on in silence for a while, but it wasn't an uncomfortable silence. And the rest of the three-hour walk, she told him about all the warm

147

places she'd been, from Southern California to Hawaii to the Bahamas to New Mexico, Texas, Florida…

~*~

Sasha saw the standing stones long before they reached them, of course. The sight brought on an elation so intense that she stuttered for the first time since she was a child, and immediately shut her mouth, embarrassed. It was extra awful because she was stuttering in Gaelic, so she didn't have her normal coping mechanisms to correct it — aside from closing her mouth.

"Th th th th there it is!"

Bless him, Seumas didn't show that he noticed her difficulty. He just nodded as he hoisted Deirdre into a more comfortable carrying position up over his shoulder.

Sasha ran the last hundred yards, barely noticing all the rocks she felt through her impractical boots. By the time Seumas got there, Deirdre was awake, and she ran for the last little bit to join Sasha and go exploring. Sasha pointed out every standing stone and named them for Deirdre, vaguely explaining that some old man where she was from knew a great deal about them.

And then they got to the largest standing stone, and as soon as Sasha touched it, she had another vision.

Flames springing up all around them. Streaks of lightning scorching the earth. Laughter that she recognized but couldn't place.

When she came back to herself, Seumas had caught her once more.

She grabbed him.

"I saw this area ringed with fire and lightning. It canna hae been a natural thing, 'twas far ower weird for that. And I know it wull come tae pass. All the rest o my visions hae. We should hurry up and find the sword and then get oot o here."

She had the creepiest feeling she was being watched. It was raising the tiny fine hairs on the back of her neck and down her shoulders and upper arms, giving her goosebumps. She looked all around, but she couldn't see anyone. That didn't mean they weren't there.

But she had come all the way out here, so she was going to search.

Seumas searched as well.

Little Deirdre was following her all around, imitating what she was doing. Sasha wasn't sure if the wee lass was really searching, but she sure was adorable.

Sasha felt all over the rocks for places of concealment, looking carefully for runes carved into the stone like in the underground castle, telling how to open the secret doors. So far, she'd seen none of that, though. Galdus's actual grave had been dug up many times, of course. She highly doubted anything would be found in there. That would be the last place she looked.

She stood still for a moment and smiled, making herself look all around and be in the moment. She had no urge at all to take a photo. It looked the same now as it did on the Internet back in her time. But it was beautiful to her.

These rocks were so old and whether worn, yet had so obviously been placed here because of the formation they made. A clock and calendar, marking where the sun was in the sky during the day and the year. Right now it was midday, so the rocks only had tiny little shadows. The real show came at sunset and sunrise, when the sun peeked through the gaps between the standing stones.

She was reaching out to touch the second to last stone when the flames leapt up. Startled, she screamed and jumped backward into the center of the ring of stones.

Behind her, she heard Seumas scream out in pain, and she turned around to see him holding his shoulder while dodging back from the flames which had appeared around the perimeter of the stone circle.

They were trapped inside, at the mercy of whoever was causing this magical fire.

And Deirdre was nowhere to be seen.

Sasha had just started to think that fire wasn't enough to keep her in here and she could run through the flames and not get too badly burned and then roll to put the fire out if her clothes caught — when the lightning started. There was no way she would survive being hit by that.

Seumas had walked over to her and taken hold of her, probably more for their comfort than anything else. He whispered in her ear.

"Ye were on the edge o the stone, even more ootside the ring o stones that I was. The fire went right through ye, Sasha. Ye were no burned. I wasna in the fire as much is ye were, and look at me." He took his hand away from his shoulder for a moment and showed her where his shoulder had been burned right through his shirt. "I patted oot the flames here, and that was what made me cry oot."

She gave him a look of anguish and sympathy. It had to be excruciatingly painful to be patting flames out on top of a burn.

At long last, their attackers came near. She could hear three sets of footfalls outside the ring, and when they got close, she could sometimes see three white-robed figures through the wavering flames. They stopped only a few feet away on the other side.

And then she heard Brian the Druid's voice, and she cursed aloud.

At first, Brian was laughing. The laugh she'd heard in her vision. How had she not recognized it? The Druid's laughter was disturbing. It was the cackling normally associated with a witch, but in a male voice. It was just... Wrong.

She felt relief when at last he stopped laughing and spoke, even though he was speaking cruelly.

"Aw, Sasha. Ye hae come such a long way, all the way from a distant future. Ye left such a life o ease and luxury. I'm verra glad ye did. And verra glad ye found love. Ah, love. A powerful, powerful force in the waurld. It is sae powerful that I will need naught else for the rest o the year, now that I have ye. Dae ye know what I can dae with that power? Och, but ye dinna. Ye hae only the knowledge needed tae be the errand lassie for yer betters. Ye dinna ken even how tae bend time intae an instrument and have yer man use it for ye, now dae ye? Nay ye dinna."

He pointed to her ring and eyed her in a way that said she was a fool to have ever put it on, then cackled some more, and Sasha wished he would quit and start talking again.

Until she heard what he had to say.

"Ye dinna ken how much I wish I could become yer new master and keep ye tae run my own errands, lassie. Ye could make a way for me tae see the future! But ye are na suited for that. Ye are already marked for sacrifice. 'Tis such a waste, but there 'tis."

Despite her resolve, she shrank the tiniest bit at his scorn, hunching her shoulders the slightest.

It was enough. Derision poured out of the old Druid's mouth like sewer water.

"Och, and I am meant tae be locked inside the tower, ye say? Tsk, tsk, tsk. Yer friend Kelsey even knows I hae the power o illusion, and she didna tell ye, did she? The two o ye lasses think yer sae clever. Ha!"

Changing into the likeness of Laird Malcomb, he laughed now again, but this time it was a laugh of amusement — which was even more dreadful than his cackling laugh of mockery had been.

But right up against her ear, Seumas made a pleased sound in his chest.

At first, this puzzled her, but then she remembered Laird Malcomb was his uncle. She squeezed him tight, acknowledging his relief in realizing his uncle hadn't been displeased with him at all, that it hadn't even been his uncle they met in the marketplace. Just another of Brian the Druid's illusions.

If she hadn't been holding Seumas, she would've put her hands over her ears. Even though she was holding him, she was still tempted. Instead, she rested her head against his chest so that at least one of her ears was covered.

He must've read her mind, because he covered her other ear with the hand that wasn't holding his shoulder. She squeezed him tight again, this time in gratitude, and he caressed her cheek with his thumb.

Their mutual comforting made Brian laugh all the harder. He laughed so loud, she could swear it was echoing off the nearby mountains. And then he spoke some more, and this time she was wishing he would laugh and quit talking. She could hear him through her covered ears, but it wasn't nearly as unpleasant.

"Ha, I hae na hatred for ye, Sasha, only envy. I'm old and wise, and I can admit tae envy. It willna save ye, this realization that I dinna hate ye, but mayhap it wull be a small comfort tae ye, tae ken that yer dying now from hatred, but from greed. Aw, only greed. I want that power ye hae inside ye, the power o creation that ye carry. I can use that power —"

He grunted. One of the other Druids must have nudged him.

He grumbled something and then went on.

"Verra wull, we can use yer power. Howsoever, it canna be harvested this day, ye ken. The moon must be at its fullest, in order for us tae take yer power. And that willna happen for a few days yet. Sae ye must stay here until then. And it would be a waste tae feed ye. Anyhow, hardship will make yer love blossom intae a greater flower than it is even now — creating all the more power for us tae harvest."

He gave his delighted laugh now, and she was starting to understand that each time he laughed, it would be even more horrible than the last time.

Well, she wasn't going to go down without a fight — or at least a negotiation. Knowing others were here who felt sure of themselves enough to nudge him gave her a little bit of confidence. It was to them she addressed herself.

"Whosoever has come here with Brian, I now speak tae ye." Remembering what Kelsey had told her, she showed them her ring. "I am one of ye."

But they all three cackled now. Aside from the fact that they were all men, it sounded just like the three witches laughing in that Shakespearean play Kelsey had dragged her to last year. And then wonder of wonders, all three were just gone, and their laughter finished echoing off the mountains and then was quiet.

If she hesitated, she would lose her nerve. After looking all around one last time for Deirdre and not finding her anywhere inside the circle of fire, Sasha grabbed Seumas's hand with her hand that had the Celtic University ring on it.

"Ye said it didna burn me. My ring is why. 'Tis touching ye now. Let's go, before they come back. This place has extra power for them. They willna be able tae keep us sae easily if we leave here."

He squeezed her hand.

"What ye say has merit. Aye, let us go."

"If ye catch on fire, duck tae the ground and roll until it goes oot. Ready?"

"Aye."

"Go!"

They took off running through the flames.

And they didn't get burned.

They kept on running, making for the cover of some nearby trees. Once they were inside the tree line, they stopped and panted for breath.

Sasha made a point of letting go of Seumas's hand.

"What aboot Deirdre?"

He looked all around.

"Wull, one thing is for certain. If they come back and catch us, then we canna help her. Sae we need tae head for home and hope that she is doing the same. We canna take the time tae look for her. For all we ken, she is…"

Tears sprang from Sasha's eyes, but she fought them back. Brushing one away with the back of her hand, she nodded.

"Let's go."

They ran deeper into the forest. The branches of all the trees hit her in the face as she ran by, but she paid them no mind. This was a different way than they had come, so she was unfamiliar with the terrain. Getting scratched up was a price to pay. Still, it seemed like a good idea to stay in the trees, to reduce the chance of their being found when the Druids came back.

Even uphill, they ran.

She stumbled over a rock and lost her balance. Felt herself falling and nearly fainted from embarrassment. But Seumas grabbed her arm and caught her before she even missed a step.

They got to the top of the hill and were relieved to be going down.

But there the three Druids were in front of them, waiting in dramatic poses. No sooner had they seen the three than the three all made gestures in their poses. It didn't make sense. They were sworn to capture and sacrifice them, not entertain them with pantomimes.

Sasha let out a 'What the heck?' chuckle, and she and Seumas shrugged at each other.

Until the trees around her and Seumas began to

move.

The branches and roots moved toward her like the limbs of animals, and almost as fast. The wood crackled and popped, adding to the horror.

Sasha yanked Seumas around to run back the way they had come, but the tree roots and branches closed them in on all sides. The two of them were inside a cage the size of a small bedroom, made of living trees. The branches and leaves were so dense that the sunlight barely came in, and even now, at midday, it was almost dark inside.

Brian was laughing again, his mocking cackle. He gave them a very serious face, which she could only see in bits and pieces through the leaves.

"Sae clever ye fancy yerself, with that ring given tae ye by yer masters. Now ye wull be cauld and trapped, while ye await yer deaths."

He cackled some more, and then the three disappeared again.

Sasha sank down to the grassy ground.

"Now I dinna ken how we're gaun'ae escape."

Seumas took his sword off his back and started hacking at the nearest tree.

"I dae."

He hacked and hacked at it.

"What can I dae tae help?"

He smiled at her between swings.

"Juist stay back and give me plenty o room. Och, aye, there is aught ye can dae. Play some music on yer flute tae give me a tune tae chop tae."

They laughed, and she did get her flute out. She had mostly played the flute when she was a child, so all the songs she knew were silly. But one came to mind that seemed appropriate: 'Whistle While You

Work.' She played it a couple times and then laughed, saying the words to him.

It was wonderful watching him work, and even more so when he laughed. His laughter made his long red hair bounce and shake along with his kilt, which shuddered every time his sword hit the tree.

And then she sobered up a little.

"Won't this damage your sword?"

He laughed some more.

"That is naught tae fash aboot now, lass. Once we get home, I can hae another sword. Look." He pointed at the tree where he'd been cutting, and she bent down to look. "Once this comes free, it wull likely fall toward us, sae stand ower there."

He gestured, and she went.

But it didn't happen that way.

Instead of falling once he cut through it, the branch reattached itself and was as whole as if he'd never chopped into it at all.

Seumas sighed and sat down on the ground, leaning against the tree he'd just been chopping.

Sasha half expected the tree's branches to reach out and throttle him for trying to do it harm, but it remained still. She joined him on the ground, and he put his arm around her and leaned her against him — and then gasped when her head touched his shoulder.

She sprang away.

"Oh! Your shoulder."

She looked down at him — and recognized the sight from the vision she'd had when she first met him. There he was, lying there stoically resisting the pain. Her tears came now, and she didn't try to stop them

"I wish I had some ice to put on you."

He reached up his hand, and when she took it, he pulled her down beside him on his other side.

"I wull rest a bit, and then we wull dig oor way oot."

They spent the rest of the day trying to get out. When they dug, the roots of the trees moved into their way. When they climbed, the trees bent over so that there was a roof, impenetrable. They built a fire out of what scrap wood lay on the ground inside their cage and tried to burn the trees, but they expanded the cage out of the fire's reach until there was no more scrap wood to burn. They had a close call when Sasha tried to break off a branch to burn and the tree reached out with its other branches and pushed her away.

Nothing worked. Nothing had so far, anyway. Ever optimistic, they kept trying until after the sun went down. And then the cold came, and the only way they could escape that was to curl up together under her blanket and his arisade.

~*~

Kelsey rolled her eyes once Sasha joined her in the dream.

"I've seen many cool swords here, but none of them are the one —"

Sasha grabbed her friend.

"Brian the Druid has me and Seumas trapped in a cage made of trees. We've tried and tried to get out … and we don't know where Deirdre is. And they're going to sacrifice us, Kelsey, when the full moon comes in three days. This is where we are in relation to Torhousekie. Alfred knows how to get here."

Sasha Drew Kelsey a mind picture of their location as if she were zooming in on Google earth.

Kelsey hugged her.

"But how? Brian is locked up in the tower."

"No, he isn't. That's just an illusion."

"I'll go into Alfred's dream and tell him Brian has escaped and that Alfred needs to bring a dozen guards and rescue you, Sasha. Hang on."

Trì Deug (13)

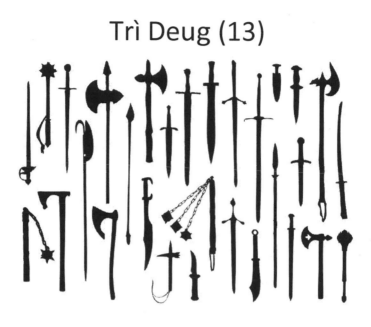

Seumas hadn't meant to sleep. He cursed himself when he awoke in the morning, the very early light of the morning. Carefully so as not to disturb Sasha's rest, he separated from her and crawled out from under their blankets to take a quick piss between the trees on the opposite side of their cage. He was crouching down to get back under the blanket when he heard something crashing through the forest.

He picked up his sword as quietly as he could and then stood guard over Sasha, whispering down to her while he tapped her with his booted toe.

"Sasha. Sasha, something is coming, wake up."

When she started to speak, he whispered again.

"Weesht. Something is coming."

It was probably an animal that was coming. It was too small to be a man. It was coming from the direction of Torhousekie, the direction they'd come from.

Seumas planted himself firmly between its approach and Sasha.

"Hopefully," he whispered, "the trees wull keep whatever that is oot just as they keep us in. Pray for that, will ye Sasha? I wull dae the best I can tae keep it away from ye, but just in case it gets through and we both die, I need tae tell ye something."

"Me tae," she said "there's no one I would rather spend my last few moments with than ye, Seumas. Thank ye for standing in the way and taking the attack. Most o the men o my time would hide behind me and hope that the animal ate me up and was full afore it got tae them."

He laughed at that, a belly laugh that was far too loud for the quiet he was aiming for. Bah, the animal could smell them anyway, what was the use of being quiet? She was so funny.

"I ken ye think I'm jesting. I wish I were. 'Tis the reality where I come from. In many ways things are better. There are more opportunities for a lass — but there's a sore lack of real men. I'm glad I knew ye Seumas."

He lowered his sword a bit though.

"An animal would hae been here by now. Animals are fast. It's taking sae long that I begin to hope…"

"Hope for what?"

"Deirdre!" he yelled. "Deirdre! We are ower here, Deirdre. Come tae the sound o my voice." He kept calling out over and over again until sure enough, there she was — a ragged bleary-eyed little girl shivering with the cold — and holding out a strange large dagger.

"He wants tae free ye," she said. "He told me tae wait until the night had passed, because it wasna safe tae be oot by myself at night, but 'tis morning now, sae here I am." She started to pass the dagger to them through the branches.

And then the weirdest thing of all happened.

The branches moved again, but this time they were moving away from the strange dagger. In no time at all, the trees had withdrawn around the dagger to make an opening through the wall of the cage, big enough for the two of them to get out.

Seumas wasted no time in grabbing Sasha's hand and pulling her up and out through the opening. She tried to reach back and grab the blanket, but he pulled her through.

"I wull buy ye ten blankets once we make it back home. If we dinna stop verra often, we can be there by supper."

He then picked Deirdre up and hugged her to him, both to thank her and to warm her up. He himself was still pretty warm from cuddling with Sasha all night. The thought of that warmed him even more, and he had to stifle the memories, lest he become distracted and useless.

They were going west toward home through a thick forest, and it was rocky and dangerous, with branches sticking out everywhere.

He stopped and put Deirdre down, sighing and looking to the north.

"We wull need tae go back oot intae the open sae

we can make better time."

Sasha followed his gaze.

"Willna they see us?"

"Mayhap, but we wull make terrible time here in the trees. Far better tae hae a chance tae make it back tae safety before nightfall. We have na chance o that if we stay in the trees."

"Verra well."

She turned to the north with him, plainly dejected and afraid.

But Deirdre called out to them, now several paces to the west.

"He says we should go this way. He makes the trees move, ye ken."

Sasha looked just as mystified by this as he felt, but he took her hand and led her after the wee lass.

Sure enough, wherever Deirdre held out the dagger, the trees parted. Even their roots moved aside so he and Sasha and Deirdre wouldn't trip. What's more, the roots dragged all the stones and twigs with them, making the path even safer than a road to tread.

With the tree limbs drawing away into a tunnel in front of them, they walked all the way through the forest. And they kept going, on and on and on over hill and dale. Whenever there was a stream, they stopped for water. Whenever Sasha had to catch her breath — which was often — they stopped for a moment and put their hands on their knees. But mostly, they walked.

The excitement wore off for Deirdre after the first few miles. After that, it was just determination that kept her going. But she clearly hadn't slept and was drooping.

Seumas scooped Deirdre up and carried her, and

soon she was snoring. The little girl wasn't very heavy. She barely caused him any pause.

After a few hours, Sasha was the one drooping — not from lack of sleep, but from pain in her muscles. She tried to explain it to him, but he already understood that life just wasn't very active in the time she came from.

"I am sae sorry I hae tae keep stopping tae stretch," she said between grunts at the pain. "Ye would think I'd be better at walking. My legs are sae long, everyone's always teasing me aboot how I should be a runner. I play tennis every weekend, and I go for a walk every day during my lunchtime. I thought those were long walks until I came here." She laughed her nervous laugh.

Cradling Deirdre with one arm, he put his finger to Sasha's lips.

"Weesht. I ken ye are trying yer hardest, and that is all ye can dae."

He started them walking again, reminding himself every few steps to slow down for her.

"I am sae grateful for yer spirit of adventure, Sasha. 'Twas different when we were children, but now that we're all grown, all the lasses here would rather stay inside the safety of the toon that venture oot this way."

What he didn't say was that he never in his wildest dreams thought he would find a companion for adventure who might also be a wife.

And there it was.

Was he thinking about marrying this woman he had just met not a seven-day ago?

Aye.

But that was foolishness.

She would go back to her time, and he was doubtless unsuited for her world. There was far too much he would be expected to know there. Fear loomed just on the edge of his thoughts. He didn't want to admit it, but the prospect of going eight hundred years into the future terrified him. He was a man. He needed to stay where he felt strong and knowledgeable.

And he would not ask her to stay here in this time with him. No. She was too soft. He was a guard who had to leave with ships and be on patrol in the caverns. He couldn't always be with her to watch over her. And no one else would understand why she needed watching over.

He chuckled a bit.

"What's sae funny?"

"Tavish's story about this being yer first time ever away from home and how it meant ye needed looking after."

She laughed her embarrassed laugh.

"Sorry about that wee white lie. Now ye ken why we had tae tell it, aye?"

He waited for her to get the jest, but she seemed not to.

"But it wasna a lie, ye ken? Ye havena ever been sae far from home — even with gang tae Florida and Hawaii and the other warm places ye spoke aboot."

There it was, her beautiful smile.

"Ye hae the right of it."

Talking on top of the unaccustomed walk was a strain for her, though, so he kept quiet awhile.

Now that they walked on easy open grasses, he held Deirdre in one arm and Sasha's hand with the other, letting himself daydream for a moment about what it would be like to go with her to her time and travel to those warm places. He let himself imagine warm sandy beaches and ocean water that wasn't so cold it hurt to swim. She had said that in Hawaii the waves rolled in and you could ride them on boards. That sounded such a marvel.

But look at her. A simple walk home — and she was not going to make it. She was limping. Her feet must be bruised because of her beautiful but thinly soled boots.

He stopped at the top of a small grassy hill where it was dry and he would see anyone coming.

"Let us take a longish rest, aye? Have us a little meal."

Sasha closed her eyes and moaned in pleasure as she collapsed onto the grass and lay down.

He set Deirdre down, and the wee lass hugged him. He hugged her back and then dug out the rest of his jerky and raisins. There were two handfuls each, washed down with the rest of the water in his skin. He wanted to be on their way again, but he saw that Sasha still needed rest.

"Deirdre, could ye keep up with me for a while?"

The lassie nodded

"Aye, if ye need tae carry Sasha."

Sasha's jaw dropped open and she looked at both of them with a wrinkled brow.

"That's ridiculous. I can walk, I just need tae rest a—"

He scooped her up and threw her over his shoulder. She weighed twice as much as Deirdre, but the weight was distributed evenly. And the feel of her against his shoulder — his uninjured shoulder — gave him a rush of energy so joyful that he wondered why he hadn't done this earlier.

They made better time this way, with him carrying Sasha and Deirdre walk-running alongside him. Both lasses had great attitudes. He couldn't ask for better traveling companions.

Unlike Sasha, Deirdre talked almost non-stop while she walked.

"Sorry I slept sae long while ye carried me, but I didna sleep at all before this. I was tae busy listening tae the dagger tell me all the things he wantit me tae dae. He talkit tae me all night long, blethering aboot all sorts o things." She patted the dagger, which she had secured through her belt expertly, much to Sasha's chagrin.

~*~

At long last, Uncle's castle was in sight.

He put Sasha down, and the three of them hurried the rest of the way home, holding hands.

Howsoever, just as they reached the castle walls, it was as if the fires of Hell sprouted up from underground.

Seumas held fast to Deirdre's and Sasha's hands and pulled them out of the middle of the fires before a ring could form around the three of them. At the same time, he hollered out to the guards on watch, whose backs he could see in a huddle, likely lighting their pipes, the fools.

"Rob, Pòl, Warrick! 'Tis Seumas. The castle is under attack, ye ken!"

To the men's credit, they moved quickly. One sounded the horn, which would bring the archers. The other two manned the gate. But if Seumas headed that way, the Druids would get inside along with the three of them.

He sighed. If he didn't have lasses with him —

But the decision was taken from him.

One of the flames transformed and became a wild boar — and opened its snarling maw and charged at Sasha.

Seumas dropped Sasha's hand and charged straight at the boar, pulling his sword from his back as he did so.

"Sasha! Run tae the gate!"

Ceithir Deug (14)

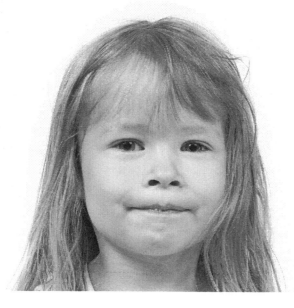

Deirdre fought her way free of Sasha's hand so she could turn around and run back toward the trees.

"He wull protect us if we go back tae the trees, Sasha. Come with me!"

As she ran for the trees, she turned her head over her shoulder.

With her face all twisted up in anger — or fear, mayhap both — Sasha was coming. And yelling.

"Come back here! We hae tae get inside! Come back here this instant!"

Deirdre shook her head no and turned back

around to watch where she was going as she ran for the trees.

Galdus was constantly talking in her head. The way he said his words was odd — like the old folks, but even more so. It was funny. And at the same time, he was sure he knew what she should do. There was no anger nor any fear in his voice. She found his presence reassuring.

"Aye, aye, tae the trees with us, lass. Tae the trees. I can keep ye safe in the trees, ye ken. Almost there. Almost there. Good lass. Good lass."

When he was happy like this — when she was doing what he wanted — he hummed and sang to her a song she had never heard before, almost whistling rather than singing. It was catchy but odd, like everything about him.

Little did ma mother think
When ere she cradled me
What lands I was tae travel through
What death I was tae see.

At last, she was in the trees.

"Go round one o the trees, lass. Put the trees tween ye and yer pursuers sae I hae some aught tae work with, ye ken?"

She did as he said, anxiously looking out to see what was happening with the battle and cringing to see Seumas wrestling with the boar. Oh good, Sasha was still coming.

Deirdre cupped her hands around her mouth in order to be heard over the roaring flames and all the yelling.

"Sasha! Hurry up! Get tae the trees and he can

protect us, remember?"

But Sasha was still using up all her anger at Deirdre.

"Lassie, I'm gaun'ae —"

Deirdre gasped.

More of the flames had turned into boars, and two of the beasts were running after Sasha. They were getting close to her.

Deirdre screamed.

"Faster, Sasha! Run!"

At the sound of Deirdre's screaming, Sasha did start running.

Deirdre tried to send her energy to Sasha, to make her run faster. She couldn't help but jump up and down, she was so anguished.

Galdus laughed. He found the oddest things funny.

"Nay matter how much ye jump aroond, ye willna hasten her."

But Deirdre loved Sasha more than she loved Galdus, so she ignored him this one time. She kept calling out to her new friend — who hopefully would soon be her auntie, if Seumas and Alfred had any sense in them.

"Faster! Run faster, Sasha!"

Galdus spoke with calm certainty.

"She isna gaun'ae make it."

The boars were almost close enough to pounce on Sasha. They would tear her limb from limb.

Deirdre burst into tears and wailed, frantically waving the strange dagger at the boars and calling him by name, wishing and never doubting he had the power to fulfill her wish.

"Make them stop, Galdus!"

She sighed with relief.

The small bushes the boars passed over reached up their meager little branches and stabbed into the monsters, making the boards bloody and tearing at them until they collapsed just behind were Sasha's foot had been only a moment before.

Still oblivious, Sasha ran up to Deirdre. At first her face was still angry, but it softened, probably on seeing her tears.

The relief Deirdre felt on seeing her friend still alive and having escaped those ravenous beasts was so great that she dropped all the decorum she'd been striving to have since Maw had first tasked her with watching her little sister. She wrapped her arms as tight as she could around Sasha's long skirts, clutching Galdus with both hands behind Sasha as she shook with sobs.

Sasha's arms went around Deirdre's shoulders, and her hands caressed Deirdre's hair.

"Aye, 'tis all right now. I'm here. But ye should hae come when I called ye. Grown-ups give ye orders for a reason, not just tae be bossy, ye ken? Now let us go back and get inside the castle where it's safe, and —"

All of a sudden, that terrible Brian the Druid was choking Sasha with one arm around her throat and the other over her mouth. He put his own mouth up against her neck.

"Ye need tae come along quiet like, if ye want yer death tae be painless. I canna make it quick, but I can give ye something for the pain. I dinna hae tae dae that, ye ken…"

While the nutty old Druid blethered on about his evil plans, Galdus's odd speech came into Dierdre's mind again.

"Well, what are ye waiting for? Stab me intae the man afore he notices ye. Go on." He showed her a mind picture of how to grip him so that her stab would be the most effective. "Now dae it. Ye must dae it now. In only a few moments, he wull notice ye. And he doesna need ye, ye ken? Sae go on. Ye must dae it NOW."

Just as he had shown her in the picture in her mind, she turned him so that he was facing Brian's side – and then plunged him in.

Sasha fell down on the ground, holding her throat and gasping, her pretty and normally pale face red and full of tears and her eyes wide. But she was alive. Still alive.

Deirdre knelt and put Sasha's head in her lap, stroking her pretty long red hair.

"Weesht. Weesht. 'Tis ower now. The danger's gone. Ye dinna hae tae be afraid anymore. I'm sorry he hurt ye, but ye should hae come when I called ye. Ye barely escaped the boars that were running after ye, see?"

She pointed to where the boars lay in puddles of their own blood, the snapped ends of twigs still sticking out of them.

Sasha sat up, a look of panic on her face, looking all around every which way.

"We hae tae get back tae the castle, Deirdre. Ye scared Brian off, but he wull come back." She grabbed Deirdre's hand and pulled her up, then started running toward the gate.

Deirdre ran with her, but she gave her reassurance.

"Dinna fash, Sasha. I stabbed him with Galdus," she held up the bloodied dagger for Sasha to see, "and he turned tae powder. His friends saw it happen and disappeared. I dinna think they wull be back. Not for a long time, anyhow."

Galdus laughed at her jest, even if Sasha didn't.

~*~

Two things happened at once after they all made it through the gate and closed it tightly behind them. Sasha and Seumas embraced and had one of their sticky gooey kisses. And Maw found Deirdre.

Even as she hugged her and stroked her hair, Maw scolded.

"Ye evil, wicked child! I hae been sick with fashing ower ye. Dinna ever go and leave again. Na withoot telling me. Ye had the whole toon looking aboot for ye. Mayhap I wull take the strap tae ye when we get home—"

But Sasha came forward.

"I beg of ye, Eileen, dinna strap the lass. She saved my life, ye ken."

~*~

Now Deirdre was invited to her first grown-up feast ever.

She twirled in the new dress Maw had made for her in the time it had taken for Alfred and the guards and Tavish and Kelsey to all return home — one full day, exactly. Everyone else was already at the feasting hall, and she was dizzy with how excited she felt.

"I love it! Thank ye sae much — for the dress and for letting me go tae the feast." She looked over where Galdus lay in the corner next to her old belt. "I wull be sae good, ye willna hae tae worry aboot me at all. I wull be just another one of the grown-ups sitting at the table with ye, I promise."

Maw smiled at her and held her hands as she knelt in front of her and then gave her a big hug.

"I ken ye wull, my sweet lassie. Ye are getting older on me faster than I can keep up with ye. I'm sae verra proud o ye. Ye were sae brave, watching oot for

Sasha's life like that. I ken Seumas is grateful tae ye as well."

Deirdre looked at Galdus some more over Maw's shoulder as they hugged again. Finally, Maw went to go fetch something she needed to bring along to the castle for the feast, and Deirdre rushed over and put on her belt and tucked Galdus neatly into it.

Now that she had him for a friend, she never wanted to be without him. She could tell she would soon love him more than anyone else.

~*~

When they arrived in the grand hall, it was just like she always imagined it would be, attending one of the big feasts for the grown-ups. Everyone was laughing and toasting and telling stories of the battle that day. At the nearest table, Rob, Pòl, and Warwick all boasted of the number of boars they had shot with their arrows. Cormac and Osgar were sour-faced at having been out with Alfred and missed the whole thing.

Her mother's friends all had their own table: Alfred, Seumas, Tavish, Kelsey, Sasha, her, and her mother. Smiles went all around the table.

Seumas looked at her very seriously and bowed his head in her direction over the table.

"I canna tell ye often enough how verra grateful I am that ye saved Sasha's life. I shall be forever in yer debt, Deirdre."

This was a little bit too much for her, and she giggled despite her attempt to put on her hard-earned decorum. Standing up so that she could reach across the table, she put her hand on Seumas's hand.

"I ken ye love Sasha. Howsoever, I love her tae. I didna save her for yer sake, but for my own. I willna accept yer service. Instead, just be my friend — and hopefully my uncle." She looked over at Alfred and giggled some more before she sat down.

Alfred smiled and nodded at her once then turned to Maw and took her hand and kissed it, and the two of them cuddled a bit in their chairs next to each other. Good. He wasn't uncomfortable with the suggestion that his brother would be her uncle. She grinned in satisfaction, knowing her mother would be happy.

Seumas stood then and extended his hand to Sasha.

"Will ye join me in the dance?"

Sasha jumped up eagerly, wiping her mouth with a cloth.

"Aye!"

The two of them walked away together hand in hand, smiling. This made Deirdre smile too, knowing Sasha would be happy.

Simultaneously, Kelsey and Tavish jumped up and stood pointing at Deirdre, or more precisely, at Galdus.

Tavish spoke first.

"There it is. That is the sword we hae been looking for."

"Yer right. Robert the Bruce's sword was a wild goose chase. This is the one we need. It was sae close along."

Tavish came around the table and reached down toward Deirdre's lap to take Galdus away from her.

She couldn't let them take her friend!

Feeling the tears come springing from her eyes, Deirdre held on to him tightly.

"Nay! Nay nay nay! He's my friend. He talks tae

me, and I'm keeping him! I found him! Ye canna make me give him away!"

But Maw took Deirdre by the arms and pulled her hands free from Galdus.

"I canna believe my eyes and ears, lass. How childish yer acting at yer foremaist adult feast. Now be quiet and let Tavish take the sword he's been searching for all this time. If ye must hae a sword, Alfred will get ye one from the practice yard."

Deirdre tried to hold on to Galdus, but Maw was stronger. She yanked him out of her belt and hands, and gave him to Tavish, who put him in his own belt. He didn't even look happy to have her friend, just determined.

Deirdre wailed.

"If he doesna even want Galdus, why should he hae him?"

Meanwhile, Isabel — Alfred and Seumas's mother — came over, smiling her sad smile.

"Deirdre, dear." She reached out her hand. "Come on. Come on up tae the nursery. Ye and me and Aodh, Niall, and Sile wull hae more fun up there together than ye could hae doon here with the grownups anyhow, with all their boring talk." She smiled gently.

Deirdre wanted to be nice to the lady who had always been nice to her, so she stood up and wiped her eyes and took the lady's hand.

But she wouldn't look back at her maw, who had betrayed her.

Còig Deug (15)

Smiling at the people they passed by, Sasha squeezed Seumas's elbow and spoke in the lowest voice she could manage out of the side of her mouth, confident that she wouldn't be overheard in the noisy great hall full of music and dancing and revelry.

"The laird was anything but friendly tae me when we met in the marketplace. Are ye sure this is a good idea?"

He gave her a surprised look.

"That wasna my uncle ye met in the marketplace. That was Brian the Druid under illusion tae look like my uncle."

That was great news if true, but she was skeptical.

"I suppose ye ken yer uncle," was all she said.

But he nodded firmly.

"Aye, that I dae. I'm sore at myself for letting that Druid's illusion fool me."

They were almost to the dance set now, and Sasha steeled herself. She was still shaken from the battle, and she didn't know if her psyche could take anymore battering, especially the kind the laird had given her at their first meeting.

They went around the last few people in the dance set and joined in, taking the hands of the people to their right and left — as well as taking each other's hand to complete the circle.

Seumas's hand felt warm in hers, and so reassuring. She relaxed into his touch.

And there was Laird Malcomb, directly opposite them in the set — and smiling at them jovially.

"Long time, Nephew, long time! And who is this vision of loveliness?"

Seumas gave her a knowing look and then turned back to his uncle, holding her hand up — a bit possessively, even though his uncle was dancing with a woman clearly his wife, by the way she looked at him — also possessively.

Seumas's voice was proud.

"This is Tavish's kinswoman Sasha. Sasha, meet my uncle, the one and only Laird Malcomb."

It happened to be the part of the dance where they all bowed to each other, and Sasha smiled and bowed at Laird Malcomb ironically in the course of the dance.

He returned her smile, and then they had a lively ten minutes of jumping and skipping and clapping and spinning and twirling each other by arms.

Seumas was a great dance partner. He led her with a sure hand, and she always had an indication what they would do before it came. Dancing with him was great fun, let alone dancing with a bunch of people who were all skirted — half in kilts. She had a grand old time smiling and making friends with everyone, and they all seemed happy to meet her.

When the music stopped, they smiled and bowed at everyone and moved on to the next dance set that was forming, with new people.

The musicians started playing again, a faster tune. It was still a set dance — all of them were — but this one involved lots of standing around next to each other and clapping while only one pair of dancers was active at a time.

Seumas took the opportunity to start a conversation that wouldn't be overheard, clever fellow that he was.

"Wull now that Tavish and Kelsey hae the item they came tae get, they will be going back tae yer home. And they will be taking ye with them. I sense this will be soon. And Sasha, if they take ye with them, I will lose ye forever. Nay one has telt me this, but I feel it here in my heart. Dinna go with them. Bide here with me and be my wife and an auntie tae Deirdre, Aodh, Niall, and Sìle. Be the maw o my many bairns and yers, who will be their cousins. I am begging ye tae bide with me and share my life. I love ye, Sasha."

She had to say one thing before any time went past at all, lest there be any misunderstanding.

"I love ye too, Seumas."

Right there on the dance floor, he held her to him

in a tight embrace that was not at all clinging. It was more… Triumphant.

But she had to clear up the misunderstanding she'd caused after all.

"I canna bide here with ye though, Seumas."

He froze for a moment, and then still holding her hand, he turned and walked with her through the halls of the castle in silence until they were out in the courtyard with the moonlight glinting off the practice swords in their bins, quite alone together. There, he turned to face her and took both of her hands in his, gazing intently into her eyes with yearning.

"Sasha, if we love each other, then we should be together. Marry me. Please. Make me the happiest man —"

The yearning in his eyes was so strong, she had to stop his pleading, had to make him understand before he went too far and felt the fool. Experience told her men didn't take well to that, feeling like a fool. And he was too magnificent of a man to feel that way. The sight of him made her nearly drunk, the way the shadows of his muscles flexed in the torchlight whenever he moved the slightest.

She stepped up to him and put a finger over his mouth gently, at last quieting him.

"Seumas, come with me instead. Ye said it yerself, there's naught for ye tae dae here. Howsoever, ye will be verra knowledgeable about this place in my time, more knowledgeable than anyone else on the site. Ye are an expert in this site, and in my time, that can be turned intae a livelihood — a good livelihood, better than ye can imagine. I promise. Please, let's go back tae my time together."

She watched his face, hoping against all hope that

he would agree. She could see the fear in his eyes, the fear of the unknown. It ate at her, but what else could she do? Her own knowledge was wasted here. No, he had to come to her time. That was the best use of both of their knowledge.

But oh, how wonderful it had been to be here for a short time. She looked all around her at the courtyard and imagined everything she had seen stretching out for miles and smiled to herself.

And then she remembered that he hadn't said aye yet, that he would come. Her heart grew anxious, and she looked up again into his eyes with the same beseeching look that he had used on her, bless the man.

He grabbed her in his embrace roughly, taking charge once more, which made her smile — but she kept the smile to herself, hiding it by putting her head on his shoulder and putting her arms around his neck and drawing his head down for a long kiss.

The kiss was all-consuming, and it lasted much longer than she'd intended. But it might be their last kiss, and so she lived in it. She threw everything she had into it, throwing caution to the wind and even pressing the rest of her body against his in blind uninhibited passion.

This is a bit too much for his sensibilities, and he drew away from her, albeit reluctantly.

She swallowed. Was this it? Slowly, she dared to look back up in his eyes again.

They were soft and tender, and her heart leapt with hope.

When he spoke, it was resignedly, but also determined.

"I will come with ye. I dinna want tae live withoot

ye, Sasha. When will we go?"

She hugged him in glee, and he hugged her back, tentatively at first, and then with strength, reclaiming her as his own. Again, she hid her smile.

"We're leaving in the morning, first thing."

"How will we go?"

"We go intae that one corridor in the underground castle, and there, Tavish can use his ring tae take us back tae my time."

He nodded.

"I did hae my suspicions about that place, but whenever I thought about it, my thoughts were redirected somewhere else. A bit o the sorcery that protects the place, aye?"

Was he testing her? She looked into his eyes and asked him that question with her own.

Seeing only acceptance there — well, acceptance, a bitter reservation, and a huge amount of resolve along with love for her — she continued on. She'd told him this much. She might as well finish. If he was to be coming along with her, he needed to know, after all.

"Aye, it probably is sorcery. But 'tis na Tavish's nor mine nor Kelsey's. The magic belongs tae the Druids who run the institution where Kelsey and I studied. They've enslaved Tavish's family for generations, mayhap the verra same way Brian said he wished he could enslave me. They send him back in time tae collect artifacts, and this last time 'twas that sword Deirdre found and calls Galdus."

He nodded, and then he looked at her with concern.

"But we canna just go in there after we tell everyone goodbye. We need tae go north toward yer clan's land — either by foot or by ship."

This time it was her turn to nod.

"Aye, that's what we're gaun'ae dae. And then we'll sneak doon tae the corridor and go back tae my time."

He pulled back from their embrace so that he could see her face and she could see his smile.

"Tavish and I did some aught a few years ago which might make that a little easier than ye would think."

And with those cryptic words, he swung her around so they were walking together back into the great hall. This time, his arm was around her shoulders, and he was holding her close to him. Yes it was a possessive hold, but she also felt such warmth from him that it radiated through her whole body, making her a bit dizzy.

As soon as they stepped over the threshold of the great hall, he raised his voice to be heard above the musicians and all the chatter.

"Sasha and I are to be married!"

Everyone took up their tankards and raised them in the air, shouting a cheer.

"Huzzah!"

Seumas waited for the cheers to die down.

"We will be going with Tavish and Kelsey in the morning, back tae their clan's land tae start oor new life together. And sae this is goodbye this evening, but dinna make it a sad one, for I am a verra happy man indeed."

And with that, he shocked Sasha by turning and kissing her soundly in front of everyone.

The hall erupted in cheers again, and everyone came to shake their hands, even Laird Malcomb. He seemed a bit flustered and about to say something a few times before just giving them a smile and hugging both of them together.

"Wull, may ye both be verra happy. I ken ye wull live long lives and be verra good tae each other and hae many many bairns." With that last line he laughed, and everyone else laughed with him.

~*~

Sasha didn't get the chance to speak privately with Kelsey until that night in their dreams, but then they had plenty of time. After a lot of laughing and congratulations and 'I told you so's, finally Kelsey got serious.

"Yes, it's so much safer back in our time. Can you imagine childbirth in this time? And Sasha, you want kids. It's so obvious."

~*~

Eileen held out Sasha's suit, and she gingerly accepted it. Determined to keep a calm face, she looked the garments over, bracing herself for the damage. Not finding any, she turned toward Eileen's bedroom, eager to go change. And then remembering her manners, she turned back to thank Eileen and was overwhelmed with just how much the woman had done for her.

"I thank ye, Eileen. Na just for laundering my suit, but for allowing me tae bide here and taking me in as part o yer family — na tae mention as yer apprentice at the weaver shop. Ye hae made my time here feel like home, and I dinna ken how I wull ever repay ye."

Eileen smiled a mischievous smile and stroked a tapestry that Tavish and Kelsey had brought her from Turnberry Castle.

"Surely ye jest. Ye are the one who convinced Kelsey tae bring me this. This is far more payment than I deserve."

They laughed together, and then they hugged.

~*~

Sasha and Seumas walked arm in arm behind Tavish and Kelsey to the sendoff Laird Malcomb had prepared for them at the east gate out of the castle town. Alfred and Eileen walked arm in arm behind them. The sendoff was a nice touch. The dance band from the night before was playing.

Seumas and Alfred at first just clasped forearms, but then they hugged.

Alfred gave his younger brother a stern look.

"Take good care o Sasha, now."

Seumas nodded upward with his chin at his brother.

"Aye, and ye take good care o Eileen, now."

They stood hugging each other for a moment and then they both nodded and separated to put their arms around their loves, the new guardians of their hearts.

Laird Malcomb shook forearms first with Seumas, then with Tavish.

"Remember, ye can come back anytime, if there is a need. Dae not burn the bridge behind ye, aye?"

Seumas nodded.

"Aye, Uncle. We thank ye, and we will remember that. Ye never can be sure we willna take ye up on that sometime."

~*~

For Sasha, it wasn't soon enough when they started on their way, but she knew Seumas needed time to say farewell. She could barely believe he was coming with her, and she squeezed his hand that was over her shoulder every time she remembered just how lucky she was that he cared enough to turn away from everyone else he loved and come with her.

There was no reason to speak Gaelic now, and Seumas had assured her he did understand English, thank God. At least he didn't have a language barrier to contend with when he got to the twenty first century.

Once they were out of earshot, she asked the question she'd been wondering about all morning.

"Is there another place Tavish can time travel? I thought we had to go back into the underground castle."

Tavish turned around and walked backward in front, and he and Seumas smiled huge.

"We need to go back down into the underground castle, all right, but we're going to need this rope." He held up a length of rope about 100 feet long, and he and Seumas laughed heartily.

Sasha put her hands on her hips, and as she did so, she had a pang of grief that she wouldn't see Deirdre again.

"Okay, obviously the two of you know what you're talking about. Would you please enlighten the rest of us?"

Kelsey already knew, though. She excitedly explained.

"As soon as we go around those trees and can't be seen anymore, we'll turn left and backtrack along the cliffs to where we can lower ourselves over. Tavish and Seumas know of a way in down there. They were supposed to block it, but they had a feeling they might need it one day, so they left some wiggle room."

The prospect of lowering herself over a cliff

terrified Sasha, mostly because she was wearing her good suit again and didn't want to get it all scuffed up. But she didn't say anything. She was determined to be a good sport. In the light of Seumas having to leave his whole life behind, ruining her suit was more than trivial. She kept telling herself that.

When they got to the spot, Tavish tied the rope around a big rock, and then Seumas held it.

Sasha had a terrible thought.

"Who's going to hold it when the last one of us goes down — and more importantly, are we just going to leave it there? Let Malcomb know we've gone down there, once he finds it?"

Tavish stepped forward.

"I'll go last. I'm lighter than Seumas, so the rock should hold me, but I'm still strong enough to assist you ladies after he goes first."

Seumas nodded and took position with his kilted rear hanging over the cliff and holding the rope to repel down to the hidden cave.

But before he could start, Deirdre came running out with tears streaming down her face and grabbed ahold of Sasha by the waist and held her tight.

"Take me with ye."

Sia Deug (16)

Sasha's arms automatically wrapped around Deirdre. And then Sasha was kneeling so that she could be face-to-face with the little girl whose face was red with tears because she was sobbing and gasping for breath. Tears dripped down Sasha's face too.

While she held Deirdre close and rocked her in her arms, a fierce feeling of protectiveness came over Sasha, unlike anything she had ever experienced. She opened her watery eyes and looked at her best friend, pleading for some kind of answer.

Kelsey came over and knelt beside them for a moment, clearly thinking things through.

And then she hugged Sasha.

"Stay here. You have made more of a life for yourself here in seven days than you did at Celtic in seven years. You're already an auntie to this little one, you have a future playing flute with the dance band — and besides, Seumas shines here. His strength and fighting abilities would wither in our time. You can tell me in your dreams if you need emergency medical care or something — and I have a feeling our masters will be in touch with you. They won't let all your training go to waste."

On hearing Kelsey's permission to stay, such a feeling of relief washed over Sasha that she cried all the more, but these were happy tears. How silly she'd been. She didn't need Kelsey's permission to stay, not when Seumas had already invited her. His was the only opinion that mattered, and he wanted the two of them to stay here.

Sasha stood up, holding Deirdre's hand and seeking out her love's eyes. When she finally found them, they looked hopeful again, and all trace of fear was gone. Confident this was the right decision, she spoke, and all doubt was removed from her mind when she saw Seumas's face light up with joy.

She addressed Deirdre, but she kept looking at Seumas.

"Seumas and I are staying here, Deirdre. We are na going with Tavish and Kelsey. Na tae bide, anyhow. We may visit there someday sae I can show him a few things," Seumas beamed at her and nodded, "but we wull live here, and I'm gaun'ae be yer auntie."

Seumas hurried over, and he and Deirdre both hugged Sasha fiercely, and then he hugged Deirdre too, and they were once more like a family.

Kelsey laughed and pulled the rope back up from where Tavish had thrown it over the cliff.

"We wull go with ye back tae the weaver shop tae take Deirdre home. That way, we wull be here for ye awhile, in case ye hae need o us."

~*~

When they all entered the weaver shop, Eileen looked puzzled — and then cross when she saw her daughter with them.

"Deirdre! Ye canna be sneaking off like this. What am I gaun'ae dae with ye?" She sighed heavily and looked at Sasha apologetically. "I'm sae sorry she ruined yer trip."

Sasha took both of Eileen's hands in hers.

"I am na sorry at all that she ruined oor trip. In fact, I'm pleased as punch. She's made me realize — we're gaun'ae bide!"

Eileen hugged her.

"Yer sure?"

Sasha hugged Eileen back and nodded against her face.

"Aye, we're sure."

Eileen backed away and held onto Sasha's hands, then looked around at everyone.

"Then I had best get ye tae Laird Malcomb straightaway."

Keeping hold of Sasha's hand, she turned and hurried toward the door, dragging Sasha behind her. Deirdre held on to Sasha's other hand and went along too, with Seumas and Tavish and Kelsey following close behind them.

"What's going on?" Sasha called out as they rushed through the castle town with everyone looking at them curiously.

But Eileen didn't answer, just laughed and hurried her.

"Quicken yer step, will ye?"

At last, they were inside the castle.

A woman who was scrubbing one of the tables in the great hall looked up and saw them all and called out to a man passing through, and he ran out of the room — and returned shortly with Laird Malcomb.

The laird looked puzzled and slightly worried.

Seumas allayed the man's fears.

"Uncle, we hae decided tae bide. I hope that is wull with ye."

Laird Malcomb broke out into a large grin and held out his arms.

Seumas took Sasha's hand away from Eileen and brought her forward into his uncle's presence. Deirdre still clung to her other hand.

Laird Malcomb embraced them all.

"Aye, 'tis more than wull with me. Much more than wull. I was utterly forlorn when ye told me ye were leaving. Ye see, I had already decided tae ask ye tae represent me oot at the surrounding castles — a different one each year – tae discuss with them what happened with Brian the Druid and what we all might dae in order tae protect ourselves. A lot o travel, and much time away from home. Dae ye wish tae take it on?"

Did they ever!

This was exactly what she and Seumas had talked about on their two journeys together so far. Their eyes met, and he looked just as excited as she felt about the prospect of traveling to all the surrounding castles together.

Her smile faltered when Deirdre squeezed her hand and took in a big breath to start talking. Sasha could guess what the little girl was going to say. She'd only just won her back, and now Sasha was rushing off without her again.

Sasha spoke to Eileen, but she held Seumas's eyes while she did, pleased to see that he agreed with her and would support her in this, as he had in everything.

"We will only gae if Deirdre can foster with us and come along."

Eileen looked to her daughter, who nodded yes vigorously.

"Aye!"

Seachd Deug (17)

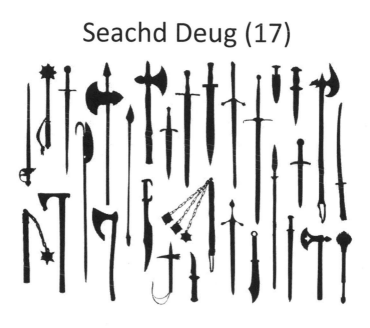

~After Alfred & Eileen and Seumas & Sasha's double wedding at the castle~

Seumas laughed his hardest as he followed Sasha, Kelsey, and Tavish up the familiar stairs into a place that was completely unfamiliar — even though it was on the same land as his uncle's castle.

Betting he would shock them all, Seumas spoke to them in English (with his Scottish accent).

"Will ye look at that? Even though ye telt me about the trailers and the cars — and the fact that Uncle's castle is gone and the ruins o a newer tower house stand in its place... even with the telling, ye hae the right o it."

Speaking quite a different English, Sasha put her arms around him and leaned her chin on his shoulder.

"If it's too much for you, we don't have to visit. We can go back right now."

Quick as he could, he leaned down and looked into her eyes.

"Ye must be jesting. I canna wait tae ride a wave on a surfboard!"

She laughed and tugged him over toward one of the cars.

He went willingly, but to himself, he could admit he was a bit afraid.

Tavish shook his hand.

"Congratulations again, and I know you're going to have the most wonderful honeymoon ever."

Kelsey looked at Tavish wistfully then.

Feeling like an intruder into their private business for noticing, Seumas turned away toward the car. He was on the passenger side, of course. Sasha had offered to teach him to drive, but for this first trip into the great unknown, he figured he'd have enough to do just looking around.

She got in on the other side and reached over and pulled up a little part of the inside of the car.

"Pull on the handle and open the door and get in."

Bless the lass, she covered her laughter as he tried to find the handle. Soon, he was inside the car with her, and she put her hand on his leg while she fastened a strap over his chest.

"Are you sure you want to leave for Hawaii right away? Kelsey will let us use her trailer. We can spend the night here and…"

After she fastened a strap over her own chest, he gently took her chin and turned her face toward him.

"Ye wanted yer wedding night tae be in Hawaii, and ye already let me hae the wedding with my family. We're gaun'ae wait till we get there."

As nonchalantly as if it was something she did every day — which he supposed it was, come to think of it — she put what she'd explained was a key inside the neck of the machine and turned it, causing a great rumble that made him try to jump out of his seat even though she had warned him it was coming. She pulled on something and pushed on something with her foot and pulled on something else, pushed on something else with her foot, and the machine took off at an unbelievable speed, making his knuckles turn white on the arms of the chair he was sitting in.

"Okay, so long as you understand my mom and my brothers will be there along with most of my extended family — and they'll throw a big party for us the first five or six hours."

It took him a few moments to find his voice, seeing as how the world was whizzing by him much faster now than it ever had on a horse or ship.

"Even sae, lass." His voice sounded shaky when it came out.

And then the car spoke to her, and he could feel his mind expanding.

Ochd Deug (18)

~A year later~

Sasha looked out the arrow-slit window of their upstairs suite at Turnberry Castle and admired her view of the sea cliffs before she laid little two-month-old Artair in the cradle that Laird Cathal had been more than happy to lend them.

She caressed their son's head and kissed him.

"Are ye full enough now tae sleep for a bit, eh?"

Seumas came up from behind her and put his arms around her waist, encouraging her to lean back into his supportive strength, which she did.

He rested his chin on her head.

"Will ye miss the view when we hae tae leave come

spring?"

She turned around to face him, and as usual when they were this close and alone with the baby not crying, they kissed and caressed each other. After a bit of that, she rested her cheek on his chest and turned again so that they were both looking out at the sea.

"I dinna think sae. This has been wonderful while we were here, but new adventures await, ye ken."

She smiled up at his handsome face, deliriously happy to be his wife and to be living a life that had already surpassed her wildest dreams of adventure and was only just beginning.

The door banged open and the two of them laughed, knowing it was Deirdre.

Sure enough, their seven-year-old fosterling barged in — but she looked much more excited than usual.

"Sasha! Come on doon tae the dock! Ye hae a special surprise!"

Deirdre was already running past all the tapestries down the orange stone hallway toward the stairs, and Sasha followed, laughing and calling out after her.

"A surprise for me? What is it? I canna imagine."

But Deirdre just giggled and ran all the way down to the dock, where a ship was unloading cargo.

Sasha looked first among the crates — but she couldn't think of anything she really wanted. Besides, she and Seumas and Deirdre and little Artair had to travel light.

And then she saw her surprise.

Her jaw dropped, and tears sprang from her eyes while she ran forward with her arms out.

"Mom!"

Oops. She was so excited, she'd spoken English. But oh yeah, Mom didn't know Gaelic, so she would have to speak in English anyway. Perhaps as little speaking as possible in front of others would be the best way forward.

Things had gone excellently well this past year, but that didn't mean rumors that she was a foreigner couldn't start at any time. Comments had already been made about her accent, but those were easily dismissed among people who remained in the same place their whole lives.

Mom was beaming a smile while waiting to be escorted off the ship.

Sasha strode right up and held her hand out, steadying Mom's disembarkation.

"How did you... Who..."

Once Mom was off the ship and safely stood on the sturdy dock, she hugged Sasha tight, rocking from foot to foot as they always did when they hadn't seen each other in a while.

"Kelsey. She got me these clothes and... I'm here for two weeks. And I want to know everything about your life. Show me everything."

When they finished their hug, Seumas reached out to take Mom's hand, but she grabbed him in a bear hug as well, which he gradually relaxed into with a soft chuckle.

After hugging Mom back, he kept his arm around her and started her walking.

"I ken ye are dying tae meet Artair. Come on upstairs. He's in his cradle."

Mom was trying not to gawk, but Sasha couldn't blame her. It wasn't every day you sailed on a ship right into a castle. And then the laird and his lady happened to be passing by in the hallway, all decked out in their finest to go down and hold the weekly court.

"Laird Cathal, Lady Meg, may I present my maw, Janice, who has just arrived for a two week bide?"

Mom curtsied and bowed her head when she was presented.

"'Tis an honor, Sir. And I thank you for taking in my daughter and my grandson — and aw, this must be my foster granddaughter. Hello honey."

Sasha started to translate, but Laird Cathal and Lady Meg inclined their heads, and he answered in English before they sedately walked down the hall.

"Wull come, and ye may stay as long as ye like."

Deirdre took to Mom right away, hugging her and even giving her a little kiss on the cheek.

"Dinna fash aboot being a stranger here who doesna ken how we dae things. I wull show ye aroond and make sure ye dinna wash yer hands in the soup."

Still being escorted by Seumas, Mom leaned back and whispered to Sasha.

"What was that she said? It sounded like she said 'soup'."

Seumas chuckled, but Sasha tapped his arm with the back of her hand. She would bet her face was beet red, she was blushing so hard.

"Nothing you need to worry about, Mom. Here we are. This is our suite. There's an extra bed in Deirdre's room. Come on in."

Artair was sleeping, but Sasha picked him up anyway and held him out proudly. "Mom, meet your grandson. Artair, this is your grandma."

Mom took him eagerly into her arms and cradled him to her, smiling the most contented smile Sasha had ever seen on her face.

Deirdre tugged on her long skirt, and Sasha turned around with a warm smile for her foster daughter.

"Aye, what is it, lass?"

The little girl looked very sincere.

"Dinna fash aboot caring for the baby. I wull watch him while ye visit."

Sasha hugged Deirdre warmly in one arm and her mother in the other, and Seumas came in and hugged them too, so that they were all hugging in a circle with the baby in the middle.

"How aboot we all take care o each other?"

JANE STAIN

Epilogue

Amber paused the paintbrush she was using to dust off some runes in the floor they'd uncovered in a previously hidden passageway. Because of a sound she'd just heard, she looked toward the secret door Kelsey had opened that morning.

Sure enough, Kelsey and Tavish were coming toward her.

In a few moments, Kelsey saw that she had Amber's attention and started talking, pointing at Tavish's phone.

"We just got the call we've been waiting for. You'll never guess who'll be here in twenty minutes!"

Amber put the paintbrush inside her little kit and closed it.

Something weird was going on. There was this one corridor that always made Kelsey's hair grow. It didn't grow very much, only a quarter inch or so, and most people probably wouldn't even notice. But before Amber dropped out to work on digs, she'd spent six months in beauty school. Once again, her old friend had come out of that corridor with longer bangs.

When she went down there just a few minutes ago, they'd been trimmed right around her eyebrows, but now they were long enough to be in her eyes. Again.

But this time there was another clue to exactly what was going on in that corridor. Tavish's hair was a quarter inch longer as well, but there was something else. He wasn't wearing the knife he'd had on a few minutes ago. Instead, he wore in his belt an extravagant long dagger.

Things were just weird enough that Amber instinctively knew she couldn't ask about it — which was a shame, because she'd love to have a closer look at that dagger. It was almost certainly a relic from a different age. It was that extravagant.

Right then and there, she resolved to get to the bottom of all the weirdness that accompanied Tavish and Kelsey, one way or another. For now, she just batted her eyelashes up at Kelsey in an attempt to be silly and make her laugh — and divert her attention from the suspicion which almost certainly showed in Amber's eyes.

"Since you've already admitted I won't be able to guess, how about if you just tell me?" She continued batting her eyelashes and on top of that smiled a big cheesy smile.

It worked. Kelsey and Tavish both laughed.

Smiling so big Amber fancied she would see her tonsils if she looked too closely, Kelsey reached down a hand to help her up.

"Okay, you win. Tomas finally flew in for a visit! He just called us from the little town nearby!"

Whoa.

Tomas was here?

All thoughts of getting to the bottom of the

weirdness of the corridor and Kelsey's growing bangs and even the fascinating dagger flew out of Amber's mind as she took Kelsey's hand and let her help her up. She whipped out her little mirror and checked her makeup, then put her hand in front of her face and breathed out, trying to smell her breath.

"Twenty minutes, you say?"

Kelsey laughed and grabbed Amber's arm and started walking her toward the exit.

"Eighteen minutes now. Come on. If we hurry, you have just enough time to get cleaned up and redo your hair and makeup. I'll help. Oh, and some more good news for you. Sasha won't be coming back after all, so the second bedroom in my trailer is officially yours."

~*~

Amber could barely contain her excitement as she watched the car drive up the road toward the dig site. She hadn't seen Tomas in seven years. She was intensely curious to see how he had changed and to hear what he'd been up to. She hoped he wasn't fat. Yech. Did he have an artsy job like hers? Or did he work in an office somewhere? She really hoped the latter wasn't the case.

She was rocking forward and back from her toes to her heels by the time the car pulled up, and she had to consciously make herself stop so as not to look silly.

The car had tinted windows, so her curiosity was still unsatisfied.

Should she rush up to the car and be the one to greet him when he stepped out? Some sort of odd hesitation made her give the opportunity to Tavish instead.

That was probably better. Tavish had been the one to invite him after all. And they were brothers. Twins. Non-identical twins, but still...

Yum.

Tomas was still tall and lean. He had long hair and wore a flowy poet's shirt that could have been made by the same person as her flowing blouse. He had a tiny hint of a mustache and no beard, thank God.

The two brothers embraced, and Amber found herself smiling wistfully at them. How nice. She was glad her own brothers and sister had never lost touch with her.

Okay, Tavish and Tomas were just arm in arm now. They had turned around, and Tomas was looking over the site. Now was a good time for her to go say hi.

As she rushed over there, she pulled up the long sleeves of her flowing blouse, just in case he wanted to shake hands instead of giving her a hug. You can presume too much after seven years, after all. She was skipping by the time she got to him. Oddly, he still hadn't met her eyes. When she was right in front of him, though, he didn't have a choice.

A handshake it was, then. She held out her hand to him.

"Welcome to Scotland, Tomas."

She made her smile as warm and welcoming as she could. Maybe he would stay a while and they'd get a chance to rekindle —

The most grating female voice Amber had ever heard came to her ears across the top of the car.

"Tomas honey, come over here and help me with this door please."

The tone was sweet and should've been pleasing, but something about that voice just hurt her ears.

Probably the 'honey' part.

Dread sank into Amber as she looked over at the woman who was obviously Tomas's girlfriend. While Amber was dark-haired and olive skinned, this woman was honey blonde with alabaster skin. While Amber was quirky and artsy and thought of herself as fun-loving, this woman was stately and imperious. There was no way she could compete with such a woman. The two of them had absolutely nothing in common except their interest in Tomas. You could tell just by looking.Kelsey had run up beside Amber. She grabbed ahold of Amber's arm, apparently for support. Then Kelsey gasped, let go of Amber's arm, and ran over to Tavish.

"That's Sulis!"

Amber hurried over to see with the two of them were talking about so concernedly.

Tavish's forehead wrinkled.

"Are you sure?"

"Yes! Look at her ring."

Amber put her hand on Kelsey shoulder.

"What's the matter? Who is Sulis?"

Tavish rubbed his eyes and put his hand over his mouth, leaning down on it.

Kelsey swallowed, still staring at Tomas and his girlfriend.

"Sulis is friends with the Druids who control Tavish."

Tomas will be available May 13, 2017.

JANE STAIN

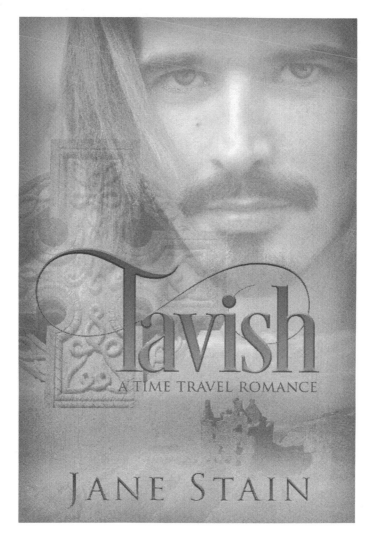

Tavish is available now.

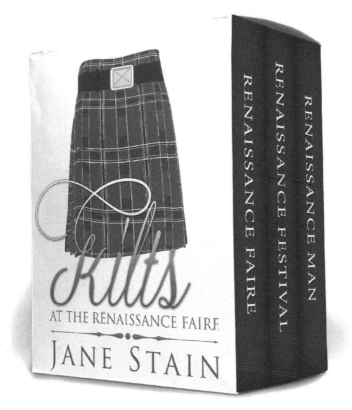

Kilts at the Renaissance Faire is available now.
This is Tavish's parents' love story.

SEUMAS (Shaymus)

Jane Stain is a pen name for Cherise Kelley, who
writes children's stories about dog aliens.

Available wherever you buy paperbacks or ebooks online.

More info at

dogaliens.com

Jane Stain

www.janestain.com

Manufactured by Amazon.ca
Bolton, ON

23985140R00136